ILLICIT DOSE OF SCARS

COPYRIGHT

Copyright (c) 2021 Dark Illusion Publishing™

All rights reserved. Copyright under Berne Copyright Convention, Universal Copyright Convention, and Pan-American Copyright Convention. No part of this book may be reproduced, stored in a retrieval system, or transmitted in any form, or by any means, electronic, mechanical, photocopying, recording or otherwise, without prior permission of the author.

ISBN: 978-1-7371753-0-8
Library of Congress Control Number:
Any reference to historical events, real people, or real places are used fictitiously. Names, characters, and places are products of the author's imagination.

Edited By: Kimberly See
Cover Design By: Diana T. Calcado
www.triumphbookcovers.com
Formatting By: TalkNerdy2me
www.thetalknerdy.com

First Printed Edition, 2021

REGINA ANN FAITH

TRIGGER WARNING

This is a dark rockstar romance for 18+.
It has dark themes, graphic sex scenes with sexually coarse language, profanity, dubcon/noncon scenes, and other mature content.

ILLICIT DOSE OF SCARS

His love was a sweet fragrance
That I couldn't get enough of
Until it turned rancid
Hurting me to the very core Burying me like a seed
Scarring my heart and mind
As he threw petals on my bruised body
-Regina Ann Faith

REGINA ANN FAITH

"All romances aren't sweet and innocent. Some are aggressive, possessive, raunchy and raw."
-Regina Ann Faith

ILLICIT DOSE OF SCARS

ONE

Journee

It is the first time I've had a good night sleep in three months. My dad and I had been going back and forth to visit my mother in the hospital. She had been diagnosed with liver cancer and was given exactly a year to live. That was a year ago.

When she was first diagnosed, my dad took my mom to her treatments, and for a while they were helping with the pain. She could still function. But three months ago, her health started to deteriorate, and the doctors put her in hospice care. When I graduated high school, she couldn't attend my graduation, confined to her bed. So my dad put in a request with the doctors to stream the ceremony. The doctors said she was the happiest on that day and couldn't believe her "baby girl was graduating high school."

A few days later, Mom slipped into a coma and was put on a respirator. That's when Dad started going to the hospital solo. I couldn't handle seeing my mom in that condition. It's not a valid excuse, I know. Most children would want to be with their parent up until their final breath, but I couldn't do it. I know Mom so it helped with the guilt I was feeling.

Tonight, I hear my dad enter my room. He comes and sits on the edge of my bed quietly, with his head down. His eyes are red and puffy from crying, and I can tell he is trying to contemplate how he is going to tell me the news. But I already know.

He lets out a long sigh before reaching out to embrace me. "Journee, your mother passed away this evening."

At this moment I feel like the air is being sucked from my lungs. All I can think about is the month before my high school graduation. My mom was beaming. She couldn't believe I was getting ready to graduate.

"I'm going to see if I can make it to your graduation," she had said.

"But you're—" I started to say before my mom cut me off.

"Sick . . . But the doctors said I'm improving and may be well enough to attend," she stated, half-smiling.

"Violet, please don't make her promises. This is hard on us as it is," my dad cut in.

"I know what the doctors said, and they said I was improving, so I'm going to try."

My dad just nodded and didn't push the matter. Mom wasn't ready to accept the reality herself.

Violet Watson fought her awful, debilitating disease with grace. She never complained and always had a smile, even on the days she didn't feel up to par. My mom knew she had to be strong for us. That was her nature. This fight, she just couldn't beat. She knew that, and prepared us the best she could. But how does one prepare for the death of a parent, or the death of a spouse?

Dad and I knew this day would come. It was inevitable. Now it is here, but it still hurts like hell, and we both cry.

A lot of emotions run through my mind as my dad embraces me. I'm angry, heartbroken, numb. I want to spend the entire week in bed, grieving. It is wishful thinking, of course. I have to grieve silently but keep moving, especially if I want to pursue a modeling career. Life goes on, as my dad always said.

"Honey, we'll be okay," my dad says as he breaks our embrace and wipes his eyes with his hand.

I don't know how process this. I don't want to process it, truthfully. This was my mom, my best friend and confidant. She was my everything, and now she's been ripped from my life.

"How . . . How am I supposed to go on without her?" I confess.

Dad lets out a shrug and a long somber sigh. "I don't have that answer, Jour. The best we know how, I guess."

My dad isn't the most eloquent with speeches or finding the right words to express his feelings. But he tries his hardest to comfort me. He leaves my room not long after. I'm left alone in the dark, to come to terms with how to live in this new reality. So I decide to escape into music. I recently found this band named Supposed Posers, and they have been helping me deal with this whole situation with my mom. Their lyrics are so honest, so real and raw. They speak to me in a way no other band has. I put their playlist on and jam out to their song "Memories," silently to keep from waking up my dad. That's the last thing he needs after a night like tonight.

The night gives way to the morning. I wake up with my AirPods still in and their song "Memories" still playing on repeat. I lie in bed, staring at the ceiling, wishing last night was a horrible nightmare. I pray that my dad will come in my room and say, "I'm going to visit your mom today. She's doing so well." But as a lie here, I know that will never happen.

Then I hear my dad's footsteps coming down the hallway. He cracks my door open to see if I'm awake. "I'm going out. I'll be back in a couple of hours."

I wonder where he is going, but I don't want to ask. I know he needs time . . . I need time.

We need to each grieve in a way that is right for us.

"Okay, Dad. I love you," I say.

"I love you too, Jour." He leaves my room after that.

I am in a melancholy mood, but I resolve to get up and start the day. Rummaging through my dresser, I find a pair of dark-wash jeans and a top. It is a white tank top with angel wings outlined in silver glitter on the back. My mom saw it at the mall one day and decided to buy it for me. She always said I was an angel sent to her by God.

Before I begin my daily search on the internet for modeling gigs, I go downstairs to get some breakfast. Cooking was my mom's forte. She could cook almost anything from scratch. That's definitely one thing I will miss—my dad can't even boil water. I consider myself an okay cook, and though I can make food to survive on, I'm not my mom . . . I wish I were. Then I wouldn't always have to settle for just eating "okay" dishes. I guess this is my opportunity to learn. Mom, be with me.

I look in the refrigerator, overwhelmed. There are eggs and sausages in the fridge, which I pull out. Then I go through the cabinets, looking for bread to make Mom's favorite breakfast: cinnamon toast. Two pieces of bread go into the toaster while I prepare the skillet for the eggs and sausages. Breakfast doesn't turn out too bad. By the time I'm done cooking, I have enough for me and my dad for when he gets home.

As I clean up the kitchen, I reminisce about the times when I watched my mom cook and sing songs. She was a phenomenal singer, making up songs to sing me to sleep as a child. Even as I was heading into adulthood, before Mom got sick, her songs put my mind at ease. They were such a comfort to me, and I will miss hearing her soft, angelic voice. Then I found the band Supposed Posers. Even though they were a rock band, I connected with their lyrics. They seemed to write exactly what they were feeling. That's how my mom sung, letting us know what was going on in her mind, whether it was about the weather or something more personal, like how she felt about me or my dad.

I can feel the tears well up in my eyes, so I quickly finish up in the kitchen and walk back upstairs. In my room, I pull out my laptop. It's black and has Supposed Posers stickers that I ordered from the their official website on the front cover. I search craigslist, as well as some other websites actually geared specifically toward modeling. I weed through the shady, explicit modeling posts. There are too many, in my opinion. But what do I expect? A lot of photographers look for models to take sexually explicit photos. Sex sells.

I set my standards early on that I won't photograph nude, and I'm going to back down from my convictions. I've had to walk off a photoshoot once because the ad the photographer posted was very misleading. I got the impression from the ad that the models would simply be in lingerie, which I didn't mind. But when I got to the shoot, there was a bed set up and the models hired were supposed to pose "seductively" on this bed — nude.

Hours pass as I sit in my room, finding a few modeling gigs that I will call in the next week or so. I go through my headshots to find the best ones to submit. But looking at my screen for as long as I have has made me sleepy. So I put my laptop away and crash on my bed.

A commotion in the kitchen wakes me up. I get up and slowly make my way downstairs.

My dad is at the kitchen table, eating the leftovers I made earlier.

"Hey, Jour, this food is delicious!" he exclaims as he chews on a piece of sausage.

"Thank you. I know it's not like Mom's cooking, but I tried."

"I got you something." He points to an envelope

on the kitchen island.

"You didn't have to."

"I wanted to. I know I can't bring your mother back. But I can give you the next best thing. Open it up."

I stare at the white envelope curiously. I didn't expect my dad to buy me anything, but who am I to turn down his gift? This is his way of comforting me, and I'm grateful. I pick up the envelope and shake it. It can't be money. It's too light. Watching, my dad has a half-smile on and this look as if saying, "Just open it already."

I rip the envelope open and stare in awe. One ticket and a meet-and-greet pass for a Supposed Posers concert. It's a dream come true. And while I'm both elated and excited, I can't help but think of my mom. If I had to choose between going to this concert and having my mom back, I would choose the latter. But that isn't possible, and my dad gave me this gift with the intention to make me happy. For that, I'm truly grateful.

"I know how much they helped you get through everything," my dad explains. "I just want to see you smile again."

I go over to hug him. "Thank you."

ILLICIT DOSE OF SCARS

TWO

Knox

The Pavilion is a state-of-the-art rehearsal space with several studio rooms. Both local and visiting bands use the space before their shows, and it is sometimes hard to even get a room. It all depends on how booked it is. During our own practices, we spend the first fifteen minutes just warming up before really getting into rehearsal. Depending if we have a show or not, we usually spend an hour or two just practicing.

Today, we are in studio 2B.

"Knox, play that guitar riff again. It sounded fucking amazing," Ezra says.

I play the riff for him again, this time with my amp turned up.

"Sweet," Reid exclaims as the last note dies.

After playing the last song, Reid, Ezra and I reminisce about our earlier band days.

"Shit, we started out playing in cafes, and clubs when they let us, and now look at us. I can't believe we get to play an arena show. We've come a long way, boys," I say with enthusiasm.

"I know. It's so fucking surreal. Hey, did you talk to Seth yet about the photographer?" Ezra asks.

Seth Felton. He found us a few years ago, when were just streaming our songs, trying to get heard. Now that he was our band manager, he handled everything—publicity, our tour schedule, the website. Everything.

"Yeah, I did," I say. "He found this guy named . . . Phoenix? Some nobody photographer who wants to be somebody. But I heard he's good, so our pics should look kick-ass."

"We definitely need new pics for the website," Reid chimes in.

We have been rehearsing for two hours every day for the past two weeks to get ready for our show. We are clearly excited. Then Ezra's cell starts ringing while we are in the middle of practicing a song. He is on the phone for a few minutes while Reid and I continue to practice without him.

When he hangs up, already knowing who it was, I ask, "What did Seth want?"

"He wanted to know if we were free to get our pictures taken before our show, and I told him we were."

"When?" I ask.

"This Saturday at nine in the morning. It sounds like it'll be an all-day shoot," Ezra explains. "You guys up for it?"

"Hell yeah. We really need to put new pictures up. The ones we have are at least two years old," Reid reiterates.

"Saturday it is," I say in agreement.

I barely slept last night. I was so stoked for our shoot today. The night after our last rehearsal, Phoenix called to tell me his idea for the shoot. He wants the band to wear all black because we are going to use the infamous graffiti wall. It's grungy, edgy, colorful, and exactly our style. He gave me the address and mentioned he was also going to call Ezra and Reid to let them know.

I have lived in my apartment since I was twenty. My parents helped me buy furniture and even paid a portion of the rent when I first moved in since I refused to get a roommate. For a while, I worked different jobs to pay my half. Then Seth found us, and now money is not as big of a deal.

My "bachelor pad," where we also have our lyric-writing sessions, has seen several parties, which tended to involve smoking weed, drinking, and some harder drugs on occasion. Those nights were all about chasing highs, never-ending hangovers, and girls I don't even remember fucking, but you are only young once, right? But most of my time in this apartment is spent alone, thinking, overthinking, and repeating the cycle.

I'm just sitting down with my breakfast—a quick bowl of cereal—when I realize that something *is* missing. I've had my fair share of one night stands and ex-girlfriends, but none of them could really handle that I was in a band. All they wanted were the benefits of fucking me, to be able to tell their girlfriends that they slept with the Supposed Posers guitarist. But they couldn't handle being in the spotlight or that I was the center of attention when we went out to different places. They couldn't handle me and all the came with being with me, but I want a girl that can. It is a rare thing that I'm asking, but she has to be out here somewhere.

After I finish eating, I go back into my bedroom to figure out what to wear for the photoshoot. It isn't too hard finding an all-black outfit—it's basically all I wear, with the exception of a little gray thrown in the mix. And our band's shirts, which I wear on occasion. While they're still on the darker side, they come in different colors, like red, blue, gray, and green.

I search through my closet and pull out a hoodie, a pair of jeans, and a pair of combat boots, all in black. After I get dressed, I gel my hair. The blue dye is fading, reminding me that I need to get it done again, but it will do for the photoshoot. It isn't *that* faded. I get my guitar case and put it by my front door so I won't forget to bring it with me. I don't know if this Phoenix guy wants me to pose with my guitar since I will probably be the only one with my instrument. It's easy for Ezra to bring a microphone since he's the lead singer, but harder for Reid to bring his drums since he's the drummer.

Driving to the graffiti wall, I can't calm my nerves. I just want this shoot to go perfectly. When I arrive, there are two cameramen, one makeup artist, and a few lighting people. I have never been to the wall, and I've lived in North Carolina all my life. I park my car, and text both Ezra and Reid to see where they are. They both say that they are still on their way. After getting out my car, I walk up to the group of people.

"Hey, Knox. What do you think?" says the guy I assume is Phoenix.

"This is so cool. Great choice."

"Where are Ezra and Reid?"

"They should be here in a few," I say. "I texted them just a bit ago."

"Okay, good. We just have today, and I want to make sure we get all the photos we can before the sun goes down," Phoenix explains.

Ezra and Reid finally arrive not long after, and we are sent to get our hair and makeup done. So much for the gel I used earlier . . . But my hair turns out better than I hoped, so it isn't a total lost.

The first round of the pictures have us standing in front of the graffiti wall in a group, as a band. I have to admit, Seth, our band manager, struck gold when he chose Phoenix as our photographer. He catches the very essence and vision of Supposed Posers. We, as a band, want to show the different sides of our personalities, something that will catch our fans off guard. We want them to think, "Damn, the Supposed Posers are back and ready to rock our faces off."

We are previewing the pictures on Phoenix's camera, and I am impressed. "Fuck. Phoenix, these are incredible,"

"Look at the way the sun shines at different angles in each picture," Ezra says.

"Having us wear all black was a great choice," Reid says. "It really made the graffiti colors on the wall pop."

"I'm so glad you like it," Phoenix says proudly.

"Like it? We fucking love it!" I tell him.

Phoenix takes a few individual pictures of Ezra, Reid, and me before announcing, "That's a wrap."

THREE

Journee

Today is the Supposed Posers concert, and I don't know what to do with myself. I'm so ecstatic. The actual concert doesn't start until later this evening, so I have the whole day to get prepared to go. A few weeks ago, I ordered one of the band's shirts to wear to the concert, and I have been listening to my Supposed Posers playlist non-stop since then.

My dad cracks open my door. "Are you excited for the concert tonight?"

"Yes, I am. Thank you for buying me the ticket," I tell him.

"No problem, Jour. I'm just happy to see you smiling again."

These past couple of weeks were an adjustment for us. While my mom was still in the hospital, my dad and I had gotten used to not having her around, but we knew she was still there. Now that she is gone . . . she is really gone. So I can see why my dad bought me the ticket to the concert. In some serendipitous way, he knew listening to them brought me comfort, and it was like I was listening to my mom sing through their band.

"I'm glad to be happy again too," I tell him honestly.

"Have fun tonight, okay? I look forward to hearing all about the concert when you get back," he says as he closes my room door.

I listen as he walks back to his room and shuts his door. He hasn't been himself these past few weeks. He's more withdrawn, less talkative than normal. And while he was never very talkative before, it's just odd seeing him so depressed.

The connection between us was never like the one with my mom. I know he cares and loves me, but he's not very affectionate. Like I need a hug every once in a while. But he tries, so I don't fault him too much.

I decide to pull out my laptop and go on the Supposed Posers website, which has new band pictures posted. I love their new look, and I'm surprised to see the infamous graffiti wall my friends in school used to talk about. They told me it was a popular hangout spot, that people liked to take pictures or add to art. I scroll through the rest of the pictures, still not believing I will be seeing them live in a few hours.

I am going to drive myself to the concert, so I decide to take a nap to be fully awake later. My dad offered to drop me off and pick me up, but I told him he didn't have to do that. I am more than happy to drive myself. He is probably just worried. Even though he bought me the ticket, he also knows what kinds of things can go on at these concerts. But he doesn't have to worry about me. I'm not going to do anything foolish. I'm not into drinking, smoking weed, or anything like that. As an aspiring model, I don't want people stereotyping or labeling me.

It takes forever to find a parking space, but I rush to get in line after I found one. The line is massively long, and rightfully so. Supposed Posers have been steadily growing their fanbase since they started out a few years ago. I, myself, didn't start listening to them until my mom got sick.

Soon we are all able to enter the arena. I get bumped into while trying to make my way to the front. I've waited too long to see this band in concert. I'm going to view the whole performance from the front row. The stage is set up with an imitation graffiti wall as the backdrop, similar to the one they used for their website pictures. There are white lights above shining down on the stage, pointing to the microphone, drum set, and guitar. Everyone in the audience is waiting in anticipation.

"Is this your first time seeing Supposed Posers in concert?" a random girl with jet-black hair and an eyebrow piercing asks, yelling over the noise of the crowd. She must have noticed me admiring the stage.

"Yes," I yell back. "What about you?"

"No, I've see them three times before. They're super good in concert."

"Three times? Lucky!"

"They are that good," she continues, "and they're

nice, down-to-earth guys too."

"You've met them before!" I ask.

"Yes, I have. I think they have a meet and greet afterward."

"I have a pass for it. I can't wait to meet them. They helped me through a tough time in my life."

"Oh, that's awesome. They saved me from taking my own life," she says honestly.

I really don't know what to say to that, so I don't say anything and just give her a halfsmile. I thought dealing with the death of my mother was a big, but almost attempting suicide?

The lights start to flicker. I can only guess that means the band is getting ready to come out on stage. The audience gets louder and rowdier.

Then Ezra comes out and steps up to the mic. "Hey, guys, what's up?"

He's tall, at least six feet from what I can tell, and is wearing a band shirt, with blue jeans and sneakers. His hair is dyed orange, and he has a lip piercing catching a bit of the stage lights.

Soon after, Reid and Knox come on stage. They also have their band shirts on with blue jeans and sneakers. Reid is tall as well, with bright-yellow hair and a labret piercing. But Knox is the tallest out of the both of them. He has turquoise-blue hair and a sleeve tattoo. I've always been curious about how long one took. Is it a gradual process?

When they start to play "Echoes," the crowd and I go wild. To be here, standing in the crowd, watching them in the flesh, is surreal. They sound so much better live. After "Echoes," they play "Memories" and "Chained"—all songs I have in my playlist. But then they play three new songs—"Addiction," "This Love," and "Undone,"—which I'm so stoked about.

While I am rocking out to "Undone," I glance up to the stage and noticed Knox staring at me while playing his guitar. I look away, not knowing why he is staring. It feels awkward. When I look back up toward the stage again, he flashes me a shy smile. I decide to smile back.

The meet and greet is inside a nearby store, and, again, the line is extensive, wrapping around the building. I have to wait for a while to finally reach where the band is. The people in front of me have signs with the band's name and the names of the individual members. The band members seem to be in awe of their fans' enthusiasm. Soon, it's my turn to speak to the band members, though I don't have anything for them to sign. I really just want to tell them how they helped me deal with my mom's situation.

Ezra is the first one I'm able to talk to. "Hi, do you have anything you want signed?" he asks.

"Umm . . . no. I just wanted to tell you that your band's lyrics helped me a great deal when my mother was diagnosed with cancer," I say. "She ultimately succumbed to it, but I just wanted to let you guys know how much your songs helped me."

"Wow, I don't know what to say. I'm glad that our songs helped you during that difficult time." He paused. "What's your name?"

"Journee."

Ezra grabs something from under the table and

sets it on the table, in front of me. "Here's our newest EP," he explains as he signs the CD jacket. "It's not released yet, so you'll be the first to hear it." He passes it to Reid, then adds "I'm sorry about your mom."

"Thank you."

Reid automatically takes the EP and signs it before passing it Knox without a word. Knox signs it as well before handing it back to me. He gives me another shy smile, and I leave the store.

I come back home, and, sure enough, my dad is waiting for me.

"Dad, it's late. Why are you still up?" I say, concerned.

"Oh, it's not *that* late," he says. "I couldn't wait until morning to hear about how the concert went."

"The concert was everything and more. Thank you again."

"It was the least I could do. I'm so glad you had a great time, Jour."

I bid him a goodnight and slowly make my way up the stairs to my room, dragging my feet on each step. I'm *so* sleepy. As soon as I see my bed, I plop down and get under my covers. I don't even change out of my clothes. I'm too focused on the idea of sleep. But as I'm settling in, I remember the EP Ezra gave me. I get up and grab it out of my bag and open it. Not only did I get to watch their concert live, I got to tell them how much their music means to me. I run my fingers over each signature. Each of their signatures are different. I wonder how long it took them to perfect them.

Knox's is the last one. I stare at it and notice

numbers underneath his signature. What the hell? It takes me a while to register that it's his cell number. Smooth move. I have to give that to him, but I am still a little hesitant to call it—even though I'm curious as to why he would give me his number. He did flash me a couple smiles. Does he like me?

I close the CD case and put it on my dresser. Knox is just going to have to wait to see if I call him or not.

The next morning, I'm staring at the EP, debating whether or not I should call Knox.

What does he see in me? I'm no slut, so if he thinks for one second I'd easily sleep with him . . .

But what if he's genuinely interested?

I decide to just go for it. I grab both the EP and my cell phone. My hands shake as I punch in his number. I take one more deep breath before taking the plunge. It keeps ringing, and just as I think it's going to voicemail, he picks up.

"Hello?" he says in a deep, husky voice.

"Hi. My name is Journee, and I . . . and I was at your concert last night," I manage to say, stammering though my words.

"Oh, yes. Journee. I'm surprised you called me, but I was secretly wishing you would.

Truthfully, that was the first time I put my number in one of our CDs. How are you doing?"

"I'm good. How are you doing?"

"I'm great. I'm getting ready to do some press about last night's concert with the band."

He pauses. "Journee, this is so unlike me, but would you consider going on a date with me?"

"A . . . date?" My head is spinning at this point, and I don't know how to answer, but his boldness is very attractive. Oh hell, what do I have to lose? "All right, I'll go out on a date with you," I finally answer.

"Great, how's later today sound? I'm free after this press event. You up for that?" "Yes, I am," I say, shocked at my boldness at this point. I can't believe I'm agreeing to go out on a date with him.

"Okay, I will text you when I'm finished with the press event. I have to go get ready now.

Talk to you later," he says eagerly before we end the call.

Holy Shit! What the hell did I just do? This is unreal. I seriously don't have a date with the Supposed Posers guitarist, do I? I do. Oh my god, I do. This is not a drill. What will I wear?

I immediately trash my closet to find an outfit. Then I pause to wonder where we are going. He didn't say. So I don't really know how I should dress. I guess I'll go the safe route—a simple top, a pair jeans, and my flats. So I pull out my light-wash jeans and black ruffle top. I rinse my hair in the shower to make my two-day-old curls look fresh again.

After I wash it, I apply Cantu to define my curly red hair, a trait I got from my greatgreat-grandmother, who was half Irish. Even though I got my hair color from her, I'm the spitting image of my father, who has dark-brown skin. I am just a light-skinned version of him. I put a layer of black mascara on my long lashes, making my hazel eyes pop. I stare at my reflection and start to tear up.

It's difficult to look at myself in the mirror some days. My eyes—I have the same hazel eyes my mom had. Seeing them in my reflection is like staring into her eyes . . . Eyes that I miss so much.

After lingering for a minute longer, I go back into my room and get dressed. I don't know when Knox will text me, but I am super excited for our date. I decide to play the EP to pass the time. There are four songs. "Wordplay," the first one, is upbeat and has a solo guitar riff, which Knox kills. "Freedom" is mid-tempo and showcases Ezra's haunting vocals, while "Sacrifice" has a drum solo to go with the up-tempo beat. The last and final song, "Muse," which is my favorite, is a rock ballad that each band member sings on. I didn't know Knox could sing. I am so used to him playing his guitar, I never paid that much attention to who was actually singing on the songs. The last song is coming to an end when my cell starts to vibrate.

Knox: *Hey, Journee, I just finished the press event. Do you still want to go out?*

Of course I do. What did you have in mind?

Knox: *Do you like flowers? There's a botanical garden we can go to.*

Yes, I like flowers. That sounds peaceful and serene. I would love to go.

Knox: *Okay, cool. Text me your address, and I will swing by and pick you up.*

I am in total shock. Am I really about to text him my address? Whose life is this? I send him my address, and he tells me that he'll come pick me up. I'm so glad my dad isn't home right now, not that I wouldn't tell him about Knox. I just don't want to have to tell my dad about him today.

I decide to look for more modeling gigs while I wait for Knox, so I pull out my laptop. I definitely have to start making some money. I"m hoping that I can get signed to a modeling agency, but in order to do that, I have to build a portfolio. I'm in the process of applying to a gig when the doorbell rings. I quickly save the application to finish later, and shut down my laptop. I make sure I look at myself in the mirror one more time before heading to get the door.

As soon as I open the door, I feel so giddy inside. Knox is smiling at me, wearing a gray button-down shirt with sleeves rolled to his forearm, partially exposing his black tribal sleeve tattoo. He is also wearing black jeans and black-red-and-gray sneakers, and his turquoise-blue hair has the bed-head look, which I don't mind one bit. It looks kind of sexy that way.

"Are you ready?" he asks me as I stand there, looking like an idiot.

"Uhh . . . yes."

I close the door behind me, and we walk to his car as he says, "You look very pretty."

"Thank you."

We're already on the road when he asks, "Have you ever been to the botanical gardens before?"

"When I was younger, I think. My mom might have taken me there. But I really don't remember," I say honestly.

"It's very peaceful and serene. I go there every once in a while to clear my head."

"I figured it would be. I need some peace and serenity in my life."

"You're stressed? You could have fooled me," Knox says with a slight chuckle.

"I'm trying to find some modeling jobs, and it's a tough industry."

"Modeling jobs? You're a model?"

"Aspiring model, I would say. I've booked a few gigs since I graduated high school."

He looked at me, puzzled. "How old are you, by the way?"

"Eighteen." I look back at him, trying to gauge his thoughts. "Does that bother you?"

"No, not at all. I'm twenty-two. Does that bother you?"

"No, it doesn't."

"Good," he says. "Because I would like to get to know you more."

"Oh."

"If that's okay with you."

"It's okay with me," I assure him. "I would love

to get to know you more as well."

When we reach the botanical garden, Knox comes around to open the door for me. To our surprise, Fridays are free admission, so Knox and I walk on in and stay for a few hours, admiring all the flowers and foliage. It is definitely peaceful and serene. The smell of the whole garden has such a calming effect, reminding me to relax and let things be. I needed this view to remind me that I need to relax and let things flow the way they are supposed to.

"What are you thinking about?" Knox asks me after a little while.

"Just how grateful I am that you brought me here to experience this," I say, smiling at him.

"You're welcome. I'm glad to be here with you," he says, reaching out his hand for mine.

I almost pull away, but something tells me to let him take my hand in his. His hand feels warm, and he starts to play with my fingers as he holds my hand. It tickles and sends a rush through my body.

"I want to see you again. I don't want this to be the only date. But I have to get ready to play some shows," he says somberly.

"I can wait for you."

"Being with me is going to require sacrifice. A lot of my exes couldn't handle it, and I don't fault them. I just wanted to let you know what you are getting into dating me."

"I understand. I'm willing to wait . . . if you are willing to stay faithful to me while you're touring."

He pulls me to his side and hugs me. "You've got

it."

I'm a little tired after a while, so I ask Knox to take me back home. During the drive, we discuss what the next date will be.

"I would love for you to meet Ezra, Reid and their girlfriends," Knox states.

"Oh, I would love to meet them," I say

"They're like brothers to me, and I don't want you to think that you're the only girl."

"I don't mind being the only girl. But since you mentioned the other guys had girlfriends, that's even better."

"Do you like rock climbing or zip lining?" Knox asks.

"I haven't done either of those things," I confess.

"Oh, which one would you like to do more?"

"Zip lining seems fun."

"Zip lining it is."

I'm still in disbelief. I just had my first date with the Supposed Posers guitarist, and now we're planning a second date. I might even get to meet Ezra, Reid, and their girlfriends. I wonder how Ezra and Reid met their girlfriends and how long they've been together. Still in my thoughts, I look down and notice Knox is holding my hand. I glance at him, and he smiles at me.

I smile back before turning toward the window. I don't want him to see me blushing.

We finally reach my house, but we end up sitting in the driveway for a while. I stare at my dad's car. I guess I have to explain where I was. It's not a big deal. I just don't want him to get some preconceived notion about Knox, especially now that I'm dating him. It's one thing to love the band—they did help me through the most heart-wrenching time in my life—but now that I'm actually dating one of the band members, that's a whole different dynamic, one I'm afraid my dad won't be too thrilled about.

I turn to Knox. "When do you leave for tour?"

"In a few weeks. So you and I will have to soak up all the dates we can before I leave."

"I'd like that."

He stares at me, inching closer to my face. He then reaches for a lonely curl in front of my eye and moves it away. I take a deep breath in, and exhale out. Holding hands and hugging are one thing. But being this close to my face and touching my hair? I have to restrain myself from leaning in to kiss him. He smells so good, and his lips are right there.

"I'd better get going," I whisper, not taking my eyes off him. "My dad is probably wondering where I've been."

"Right." Knox takes a breath and pulls back. "I'll call you in the next few days to let you know if everyone is up for zip lining."

"Thank you. I had a great time," I say before opening his car door to get out.

"Me too. We'll speak soon, okay?"

"Okay."

I get out of his car and walk up to my front door. I fumble around for my keys and look back to see if Knox is watching me. He has already pulled away. Maybe he has somewhere else to be. I finally open the door and enter the house.

My dad is on the couch, watching TV. I try to sneak past him and go to my room, but he stops me.

"Journee, where were you? I tried calling you."

"I went out on a date," I confess.

"A date? With who?"

I knew I would eventually have to tell him . . . I just thought it would be after Knox and I had a few more dates under our belts. "His name is Knox. He plays guitar for Supposed Posers," I tell him honestly.

"The band you like?" he questions.

"Yes. We met at the concert."

"I don't know about this, Journee," my dad says, concerned. "Dating someone in a band…Rock stars have bad reputations. I shouldn't have to tell you that."

"Dad, Knox isn't like that," I reason.

"Well, I want to meet him."

"He's getting ready to tour soon."

"That's no excuse. If he's dating you, I want to meet him."

I suck in a breath through my teeth. "Okay, Dad."

My dad doesn't say anything else and goes back to watching the TV. That's my cue to head to my room.

I don't want my dad to meet Knox before we have our second date. I'll introduce Knox to him on my terms, when I'm ready, no matter how dead set he is on meeting him.

A few days had already gone by when Knox finally texted me to set a date and time to go zip lining. He said his band mates were stoked to go and had called their girlfriends straight away to see if they could come.

Being on tour, he explained, there isn't really too much downtime in between shows. They are able to go do smaller activities, but even that is hard. They usually end up getting bombarded by fans wanting their autographs or wanting to get a picture with them.

I wake up early on the day of the date. It's supposed to be sunny, in the upper seventies, so I decide to wear my black capris and a short-sleeved crop top that hits right above my waist. I go with my black chucks to complete the outfit, and I let my red curls hang loose, giving me that "kind of messy but somewhat tame" look.

Knox picks me up around noon. He has on a black muscle shirt, "I'm the echo in your mind" written in white letters across the bottom hem of one sleeve. I climb into the car and listen to one of the band's songs Knox has playing.

"This is a rough demo of one of our new songs, called 'Secrets,' " he says as I buckle my seatbelt.

"Oh, I love it. It sounds different from your other songs."

"Yeah, we wanted to experiment," he says, pulling out of the driveway. "I'm glad you like it."

"I'm kind of nervous. I've never zip lined before," I confess.

"Oh, it's fun. Don't be scared." He pauses. "Are you afraid of heights?"

"No, not really. But I have this fear the rope will break while I'm in the air."

"I see. But trust me, you have nothing to worry about," Knox reassures me.

We finally arrive at Zip Thru the Line. It looks like

a huge forest with a lot of luscious tall green trees with zip lines connecting most of them. Some have wooden bridges for people to walk across to get to the zip lines. Standing at the end of one bridge is a guy connecting people's harnesses. Just watching people hurtle through the air makes me want to reconsider. But I am already here, and I can't turn back now.

"Ready?" Knox asks as he grabs a baseball cap from the glove compartment and tosses it onto his semi-damp hair.

"I guess . . ."

"You okay? You're not having second thoughts, are you?"

"Well, umm, no," I lie, pushing down my doubts.

Knox sends a quick text to Ezra and Reid to see where they are as we are walking to the entrance, but he spots them sitting on a nearby bench. "Hey, man," he says.

"Took you long enough," Ezra says. "Don't worry, we already paid for you guys."

"Thanks," Knox says as he pulls me to his side. "You remember Journee, right?"

"Yeah. How are you doing, Journee?" Ezra asks. "Nice to see you again."

"I'm fine. Thanks for asking," I reply.

"This is Willow and Sarai."

"Hi, it's nice to finally meet you. I'm excited to know that I'm not the only girl," I say honestly.

Willow has pale skin and dark eyes. Her hair is black, cut in a short bob. She has on one of the band shirts, with flare jeans and sneakers on. Sarai has tan skin and brown eyes. Her hair is also black, but it is long. She also is wearing one of the band shirts, with bootcut jeans and sneakers.

"It's nice to have another girl join the group," Sarai says.

"Oh, of course. The more the merrier," Willow agrees.

All of us walk inside Zip Thru the Line, Ezra and Reid walking ahead of us, holding their girlfriends' hands. Seeing this, Knox immediately grabs my hand and pulls me close to his side again. We linger back a little so we can have some privacy.

"How did they meet?" I finally ask Knox.

"Both Sarai and Willow were at our very first shows. They were both seventeen at the time and snuck out to go to our gigs," he explains.

"Oh, so they're rebels? I like them already," I smirk.

"Basically. When Ezra and Reid met Sarai and Willow, they were very smitten. Ezra with

Willow, Reid with Sarai, and vice versa .

So flash forward to one of our recent gigs. Willow and Sarai showed up. They had a picture they took with Ezra and Reid from that first show, and the rest was history, as they say," he continues.

"Oh, wow. That's awesome."

"Hey, Knox, stop being so anti-social," Reid says, calling back to us.

Ezra also glances back. "Yeah, join us."

Knox and I rush to meet up with the rest of the group. I didn't realize how far back we were trailing behind them until we had to catch up to where they are.

We all decide to try the beginner zip line course, even though the guys had been zip lining. They are very considerate of us girls, who never zip lined before. I watch as Sarai and Willow are getting their harnesses put on and connected to the line.

I watch as Willow and Sarai zip away, letting out bloodcurdling screams, I turn to Knox.

"I don't think I can do this."

"It's up to you. But Ezra did pay for us to get in here, you know?" Knox says.

"When you put it that way . . . I guess I'll try."

"Are you going?" the guy fastening the harnesses asks me.

I look back at Knox and the guys, who are also waiting for me to make my decision. I'm scared shitless, but I decide it wouldn't be fair to not go, since Ezra did pay for me.

"I'll go," I finally tell them.

"Hell yeah," Knox says.

He kisses me lightly on the cheek, and his lips are so soft as they graze my cheek, sending an electric current through my entire body. Holy shit. If a light peck can make me feel like this, I can't imagine what a full-on kiss would do to me. I shake off the thoughts as the zip line employee connects my harness to the line. As soon as I am fully connected to the line, I look back at Knox and the guys. They give me a thumbs-up. I finally push myself off to fly through the trees, hearing the guys clap behind me.

After I finish, the girls are waiting for me on

the platform. Sarai and Willow are drinking water I'm assuming they got from Ezra and Reid. Willow hands me a bottle of water as I approach her. Soon the guys join us on the platform.

"It wasn't that bad, was it?" Knox says.

"No, not too bad," I answer. "What did you girls think?"

"It was amazing. The wind through your hair as you zipped through the trees… There is no other feeling like it in the world," Sarai states.

"Are you sure?" Willow says, nudging her shoulder.

"Oh, Willow, get your head out of the gutter," Sarai responds.

Ezra, Reid, and Knox start to laugh. Then we chat about the day and the guys' upcoming shows. Soon it's time for us to leave.

"It was nice meeting you guys again," I tell Ezra and Reid.

"Likewise," Ezra responds.

"We definitely need to keep in touch," Sarai says.

"You'll be at the shows, right?" Willow asks.

"Not this time around," I say somberly, glancing at Knox.

"Don't worry. She's not going anywhere anytime soon," he says confidently.

"Staking your claim on her already?" Reid chimes in.

"Don't you know it," Knox answers.

Knox and I leave first. He drops me off at my house and promises he will call me every other day while on tour.

FOUR

Journee

I invite Knox to my house for dinner to meet my dad for the first time. They haven't been formally introduced since Knox and I started dating a few months ago. I wanted to make sure we would last more than two weeks before I introduced him to my dad. But those two weeks ended up turning into a few months because Knox has been busy, performing shows with his band. It wasn't until Knox finally got a break in his schedule that I was able to make plans.

My dad and I agreed to order in because, truthfully, I didn't have time to look up a recipe and learn to cook it. It's times like this I wish my mom were still alive. I straighten up the dining room in preparation for Knox's arrival. When I come downstairs, my dad is in the living room, on the couch, watching football.

"I ordered the food. It should be here in a few hours," my dad says. "You look beautiful, Jour," he adds. I opted to wear a multi-colored maxi dress and ballet flats.

"Thank you," I say. "I really hope you like Knox.

He's a wonderful guy."

"I'm sure I will. As long as he treats you right and you can love him, he's okay with me."

My dad flashes me the biggest grin before I head back to the dining room.

As I proceed to check to see if it needs any last-minute touch-ups, the doorbell rings.

"I got it," my dad yells to me in the dining room.

My dad opens the door, and, from where I stand, all I can see is Knox's turquoise-blue hair. When he steps inside, I take in the rest of his appearance—a fitted black short-sleeved shirt, gray-and-black striped slacks, and black Converse sneakers.

"Hi, Mr. Watson. I'm Knox."

"It's good to finally meet you, Knox. Journee said you were busy, performing shows," my dad says as he goes to shake Knox's hand. "Call me Myles."

"Yes, I was super busy with shows, but it's calmed down some now. I'm glad to finally get to meet you."

"Come on in and have a seat on the couch. I've just been watching football. Journee's in the dining room."

"I'm coming," I yell.

"Take your time. Babe, it's not rush," Knox yells back.

After a while, the doorbell rings again, and my dad rushes to the door. "It's our food," he says.

Knox and my dad come into the dining room and set the take-out bags on the table. My dad heads back to the living room, and Knox hugs me. He purposely lingers just so I can feel his bulge press up against my front.

"Later," he whispers in my ear, squeezing my ass.

When he returns to the living room, I start to pull out the food and set up the table. I bite my lip, fantasizing about all the naughty things Knox and I will do after dinner. I can't wait for desert.

I call the boys when everything is ready to go.

"Thank you for setting the plates," my dad says as he sits down beside me.

Knox opts to sit on the opposite end of the table, right across from me. I look up at him as he flashes me a smirk. My eyes narrow, as if to say to stop teasing me, but he just runs his leg up mine. I gasp, a tingling sensation growing between my legs. Shit. This is going to be a long dinner.

"So, Knox, did you grow up here, in North Carolina?" my dad asks, starting his interrogation.

"Yes, born and raised here. I went to Meadows Bay High School," Knox says, a hint of nervousness in his voice.

"Meadows Bay High School? That's on the other side of town, right?"

"Yes, sir. It is,"

"Wasn't there a student there that almost shot up the school a few years back? I remember hearing that on the news," my dad asks, concerned.

"Oh . . . that was just some foreign exchange student. It was a scary time for us all."

"Oh . . . I see. What made you start your band?"

"I started my band right after I graduated. I had no plans of going to college. It wasn't for me. So I decided to start a band," Knox tells him, confidence returning.

"Journee has been raving about your band ever since she found you guys. You helped her through the most painful time in her life, and for that, I want to thank you."

When we finish dinner, my dad decides to excuse himself, claiming to be tired. "It was a pleasure meeting and getting to know you, Knox," he says.

"Likewise, and don't worry. Your daughter's in good hands, sir," Knox replies.

My dad then heads up the stairs to his room. I'm still finishing up the little bit of food I have left when Knox gets up and comes to my side of the table. He pushes my chair back against the wall and kneels down in front of me. I gasp with lustful excitement as he begins slowly rolling up the bottom of my maxi dress to my hips. He pulls down my panties to my knees. Oh my god. What is he thinking? My dad is just upstairs. Knox straddles my lap, my dress bunched up between us. He grabs my hips and pulls me forward until they are slightly off the front of the chair. I let out a soft moan as he slides his dick inside me and gradually starts humping me.

"Fuck . . . we're going to break this chair," Knox says when the chair starts squeaking.

"Wait . . . wait . . ." I say, panting, almost out of breath, as he continues to ride me. "Let's move to the floor."

Knox gets off of me, stands in front of the chair, picks me up, and lays me on the rug. He repositions himself between my legs and slides back in. The pressure of his dick feels like a dream, warming my insides. He captures my lips, and our tongues become tangled with one another, intertwined together. We eventually discard all our clothes, and each time I'm tempted to scream Knox's name in pleasure, he points upstairs. So we continue quietly going at it, laughing at how ridiculous it all seems.

Knox must have carried me up to my bedroom after we finished. I smile to myself as I think about what Knox and I did last night, and wish he were in the bed with me right now.

I hug my pillow as my thoughts drift to places too explicit for me to utter. My phone starts to vibrate on my night stand. I crawl over my covers, to where my night stand is, and grab my cell.

Knox: *Morning beautiful. I wish I could stay and continue fucking you until the sun came up. You captivate my mind. And that body of yours…Damn, girl.*

I smile at Knox's text. He captivates me too. I love that he loves and wants me. I never felt this way with any of my past boyfriends.

Babe, I wish you could have too. Hugging these pillows don't work so well.

Knox responds with an "LOL," and I can hear him laughing in my head. His laughter is like medicine to my soul. We laugh and joke a lot, especially during sex, like last night, which makes it a hundred percent more pleasurable.

I put my cell back on my night stand and slide back under my covers. If Knox can't be with me right now, I'll just force myself to dream of him. As I am about to close my eyes and drift to dreamland, my dad enters my room.

"Hey, Journee. We need to talk," he says, his voice serious. "I have something very important to tell you."

I sit up on my bed, confused. Does he know? Oh shit, I hope not. That would be majorly embarrassing.

"What's up?" I say, nervous and possibly feeling like I'm going to pee my pants.

"I've decided to move to South Carolina. I already handed in my two weeks' notice."

So he doesn't know about last night. A wave of relief washes over me, but that quickly turns into disbelief and worry. "Move? Now? Why?"

"I thought a lot about this while your mom was still in the hospital. When she finally passed away, I realized I couldn't stay here. It's too painful. The memories we made here as a family are special to me, but losing her . . . I don't want to remember. I want to start fresh, rebuild, and create new memories."

I can't believe my dad wants to just up and leave. I sort of understand his reasoning, but he could have discussed this with me before deciding everything.

"What about me? Dad, I'm just starting out, still building my portfolio," I tell him. "What about Knox? I can't just move now."

"You are just starting out with your modeling

career. You haven't booked a lot here.

Maybe when we move, things will pick up for you."

Now I'm angry. "You don't know what I have or haven't booked. And Knox? I'm just supposed to dump him and move to South Carolina just because you can't deal with things here?

What! Are you going to run every time something is painful or hard?"

"Journee, that's not fair."

"What's not fair is you deciding to move without consulting me first. Like *I* didn't matter. It's all about *you*."

"I want us to build a new life, start in a new place, to alleviate our pain."

"Who said I was still grieving about it, Dad? I choose to move forward."

"How dare you want to forget your mother's memory!" my dad says, shocked.

"It's not me who wants to forget! It's you! You're so quick to want to up and leave," I snap back.

My dad turns around and leaves my room. I'm infuriated with his decision, and I refuse to leave—not now. I text Knox to meet me at Books on Books, a local bookstore. I grab my car keys off of my dresser and head out the front door. Once I reach Books on Books, I go inside and claim an empty table toward the back, by the windows. It's a few minutes before Knox comes walking around the bookstore. I wave him down.

"Hey, babe. What's up? Your text sounded urgent," Knox says as he sits across from me.

"I have some bad news."

"What is it? You're scaring me."

"My dad wants to move," I say bluntly, "but I don't want to go."

"Move? Why?"

"Because of my mom. He says it's too painful to stay here."

"Oh . . . Well, if you don't want to go, you could move in with me," Knox offers.

"Really?"

"We've been dating for a few months now anyways. It's about time, right?"

"Let me think about it. I'll talk this over with my dad. That's a huge step."

"I totally understand. Take as much time as you need. I'll be here no matter what you decide," Knox reassures me.

We both leave the bookstore not long after. On the drive home, I try to think things through. Am I ready to take that step? I love him and want to be with him, but is that enough to convince my dad? I really don't want to pack up and move.

Once I reach the house, I go up to my room to process everything and think about what I'm going to say to my dad. He should have cooled down by now, and I don't want to wait to talk to him, in case he reveals even more unexpected plans to me.

I enter his bedroom and find him reading a book. "Dad?"

He sets the book down. "Yes, Journee?"

"I'm sorry about earlier," I tell him. "I didn't

mean to snap at you."

"It's okay. And I'm sorry I just sprung this on you without any prior notice."

"Knox asked me to move in with him," I say nonchalantly, deciding to get it out in the open.

"Oh, really? And what did you say?"

"I told him I would talk to you first."

"I can't force you to move with me if you don't want to. But you are all I have."

"Not fair. Guilt tripping me is not going to work."

"It looks like you've already made up your mind."

"I have. It was more me wanting to tell you my decision."

"You're eighteen. You aren't a little girl anymore. I guess I have to accept that."

"And you have to also accept the decisions I make."

"I don't know what else to say. I will miss you terribly," my dad says despondently. "But I have to let you go eventually, and I guess that time is now."

"Dad, I love you, and you know I wouldn't make this decision if I wasn't sure about Knox and wanting to be with him," I reassure him.

"I know."

"Thank you for understanding."

My dad doesn't say anything else after that, so I leave him to his thoughts and go back to my room to update Knox.

Knox, Reid, and Ezra all helped me move my things into his apartment. My dad didn't really want to intrude. Although I think he accepted my decision to live with Knox, deep down, I'm sure he still really wants me to go with him. So it was easier for him to distance himself from the whole moving in process. He also probably didn't want to say anything he would regret and have to take back later.

It took two weeks to finish moving me into Knox's apartment. During those two weeks, we also went shopping for house decor to make the apartment look more like a couple lives here instead of like a bachelor pad, starting with the kitchen and living room.

"Is this your first time living with a girl?" I ask Knox while we are getting things organized.

"Yes, it is, but I know I wouldn't want to take this step with anyone else."

"Oh . . ."

"Don't worry about your father. I know you want to please him, but you *are* eighteen. You have a right to make your own decisions."

"I know. And you're right," I say. "It is *my* life, and I can definitely make *my own* decisions. I just worry about him. This seems so spontaneous of him just to pick up and move."

"Grief hits everybody differently. You have to respect his decision, just like he has to respect yours."

After the kitchen and living room, we move to work on the bedroom. We both decide on a black-and-silver comforter set, and we put some solo pictures of Knox from his concerts and some of my modeling pictures in frames. We hang them around our bedroom. To put above our bed, we found a beautiful mosaic painting that had a hidden "K" and "J" woven into the design.

Once we saw it, we knew we had to get it.

Standing on the bed, trying to hang up the painting, I turn to Knox next to me. "It's coming along."

"It certainly is," Knox says as we step back to admire the painting.

We stand there, on the bed, staring at the painting, for a few more minutes. Then all of a sudden, I'm laid flat on the bed, with Knox on top of me.

"What the—"

"We have to break the bed in," Knox says as he kisses my neck.

"Oh, really?"

Ezra and Reid left a while ago, so it's just Knox and me. Maybe breaking the bed in isn't such a bad idea.

On my dad's last day of work, his job throws him a going-away party. He wants me to accompany him, so I went shopping for a new outfit to wear to the party, even though I didn't really need to buy new outfit.

"I'm glad you decided to come," my dad says while driving us. "It means a lot to me."

"No problem. It's the least I can do. After all, it will be one of the last times I'll be seeing you before you leave."

"You sure you don't want to come with me?"

He glances at me, but I just give him a puzzled look, wondering why he's still trying to change my mind. "I didn't think so." He's silent after that.

The party is a bunch of his coworkers. The room is decorated with multi-colored streamers and balloons that have the company logo on them. Two male workers are chatting it up with my father about his plans, and a few of his female coworkers had given him a few gifts. They also brought a celebratory cake to commemorate all the years he has been with the company. Some of his coworkers ask me a few questions as well. I try to answer as honestly as I can while trying to keep them from digging deeper into my personal life. I don't want them to try to convince my dad that I'm not able to make the decisions I made because I'm only eighteen.

The morning before my dad is set to leave, he decides to visit Mom's grave. He wants me to come with him, of course, which I understand. I haven't been to the gravesite since the funeral, so I'm curious see how it looks now that they have the inscription on her tombstone.

"It's so weird visiting after all these months," my dad says as we stand in front of it.

I look down at the plaque. "The inscription is

beautiful."

Gravesites usually freak me out. There's just something about a large grassy field full of tombstones, though I do notice several arrangements of beautiful flowers on various graves, which calm my nerves a bit. I stand next to my dad, holding on tightly to his arm.

"I really miss you, Violet," my dad says, talking to Mom. "You were everything to me and our family. I had to make a few hard decisions that I didn't want to have to make, but I did. I'll be moving, and I know it comes as a shock, but I can't live here, in this town, without you. It's lonely—a constant reminder of your passing. I hope you understand."

A gust of wind blows through the cemetery. My dad and I look at each other. That was a sign. Mom is okay with it. She understands.

"Oh, and don't worry about Journee," he continues. "She's found a good guy named Knox, and she's decided to move in with. Truth be told, I was hesitant at first, but I have to trust her judgment. She's growing up right before my eyes. It's scary, but I know we instilled values in her so she would know how to make sound decisions for herself."

I stand there, listening to his speech, and tears start to fall from my eyes. What will life be like without him? Even though we have our differences, I still will miss him. I'll miss his advice and guidance.

My dad and I embrace as we stand in front of my mother's grave, knowing that our lives will never be the same.

ILLICIT DOSE OF SCARS

FIVE

Knox

It's been a month since Journee and I moved in together. She was very emotional the first few weeks. She couldn't stop crying. I think it was a mixture of missing both her parents and not knowing what to expect living on her own, let alone with a guy. Plus, my apartment is also where the band writes our lyrics, and Journee isn't used to our pre-session routine or what we do to wind down after.

"Sing the verse again, Ezra," I say during one of our meetings. "I think I have a riff to go with it."

Ezra does, and it's pure perfection. I write down the notes for what I have in mind, but I'm not going to reveal anything until we can get back to the Pavilion for practice. Meanwhile, Ezra adds to his own sheet, writing more lyrics or changing up the ones he already has.

"Hey, guys," Journee says as she comes out of the bedroom, "I hate to be a bitch, but I'm trying to sleep."

"Sorry, babe. We're almost finished." I glance up at her. "Come here for a second."

Journee has lacy black boy shorts on and a black-

and-white polka dot tank top. Her red hair is pulled up in a high ponytail, while her curls cascade down her forehead. This is her usual bed attire for like the first five minutes, before I get her in her birthday suit. She turns me on each and every time she wears them. So it is always a non-stop rendezvous.

She comes over and sits on my lap. My cock starts throbbing against her ass cheeks. I can't wait until Reid and Ezra leave. I'm definitely going to tap this sexy piece of ass as soon as they are gone, and I think they know it. Reid and Ezra take one look at us, then at each other.

"Hey, we'll finish up another time," Ezra says, standing up.

Reid does the same. "Yeah, we'll leave you two alone."

Both of them pack up their stuff and hurry out the front door.

Journee faces me and looks in my eyes. "I didn't mean to ruin your practice time."

"It's all right." I slide my hands underneath her tank and caress her breasts. "We were almost finished anyway."

She lets out a sensual moan as I take her tank top off, exposing them. I take her nipple into my mouth and began to suck on it. My hands move downward from her breasts, until they reach the top of her shorts. Then I slide inside and start massaging her clit. Her moans get louder.

"Oh god, Knox," she pants as I begin finger-fucking her.

I take my hand from inside her, pick her up, and

bring her back to our bedroom. I lay her on our bed. I slide her boy shorts to the floor and continue torturing her with my fingers. After a while, she's good and ready for my cock. I kiss her, sucking on her tongue. She's nearly breathless now, just waiting for me to take her.

"Please, baby," she says in between kisses.

I grab a condom off of my night stand, but Journee snatches it from me. She rips it open, takes my cock in her hand, and slips the condom on.

"Impatient, are we?" I say, laughing.

"Damn it. Just come on already."

I position myself on top of her and slide into her. She lets out a sigh of relief as I start to fuck her like she's been waiting for me to.

After we finish, I ask her if she wants to try a different kind of high.

"What do you mean?"

I get up off the bed and look through my dresser drawer to pull out a bag of weed.

I show it to her as she sits up. "We usually smoke this before and after practice. It really helps us get into zone and calm down after we practice,"

"I don't know. I've never smoked weed before," she says honestly.

"Babe, I wouldn't make you do anything that would hurt you. Try it just once."

"I don't know, Knox."

"Please? For me," I plead with her.

"Oh, okay. But only this once."

I roll a joint and start smoking it. I take a few puffs, then pass it to her. Journee's hesitant at first, but then she takes the joint between her lips and inhales. She coughs as she passes it back.

"Are you okay?" I say, chuckling.

"I'm okay," she manages to get out. "You guys smoke this every time during your practices?"

"Without fail."

We—mainly me—sit there, smoking that one joint until it's finished. After that, we lie down side by side, my hands massaging her breasts. Luckily, she doesn't mind. At one point, she reaches underneath the covers, grabs my cock, and starts massaging it. We lazily caress each other until we drift off to sleep.

The sun is barely up when I wake up to Journee's curly hair in my face smelling like one of those fruity drinks you get at a bar. I start to play with a stray strand while she's nestled close to me. This girl is so fucking amazing. Sex with her is always mind-blowing, and I can't believe I got her to try weed for the first time last night.

Journee starts to stir. "Hey, handsome," she whispers, not quite awake but getting there.

"Babe, you're such a badass," I tell her.

"Badass? Why?"

"You smoked your first joint last night, remember?"

"Yeah, I don't know if that qualifies me being badass though," she says.

"In my eyes, it does."

"Well, okay . . . Hey, listen. I have a photoshoot that I booked a few weeks ago. And I have to start getting ready for it."

"Oh, that's awesome. I'm so proud of you."

"Thank you. I need to keep building my portfolio so I can get signed with an agency."

"It'll happen. I have faith in you," I tell her. "You are extremely sexy. I don't know why a photographer wouldn't want you as one of their models."

She raises her eyebrows. "You're just saying that because you're fucking me."

"You're sexy even when I'm not fucking you. So, no, that's not why."

Journee rolls her eyes and moves to sit on the edge of the bed for a minute. "Can I wear your band hoodie?"

"Why even ask? You know you can. What's yours is mine . . . what's mine is mine, and you belong to me."

"Oh, really?" She laughs at what I said, though I can tell by the look on her face she thinks I'm joking. I'm not.

I just watch her. Journee's even more beautiful when she's smiling. But she doesn't have a clue that I'm dead serious.

Journee finally gets up off the bed and goes into our bathroom to take a shower. While she's in the shower, I text Reid and Ezra to see if they want to have a little get-together at my place tonight. They both ask if Journee is going to be there, and I tell them she is going to a photoshoot. They both text something along the lines of "Hell yeah!" It's been a while since we actually had "guy time" outside of band practice. I can't wait for our little get-together.

"I heard your phone buzzing while I was drying off," Journee says, coming out of the bathroom.

"Oh, yeah. Just planning a little get-together with the guys," I tell her vaguely.

"You deserve some guy time. I know, with me living here, it's kind of cramping your style. You're used to having the apartment all to yourself."

"Thanks for understanding, but I wouldn't say you cramp my style." I smirk at her. "You give my cock a cramp every once in a while though."

"Shut the fuck up." Journee playfully smacks my arm.

"Well, it's true."

She's about to hit me again, but I block her swing and kiss her. Journee pulls back after a while because she knows where this is going to lead. "I have to go. It's a two-hour drive to the photoshoot."

"Yeah, yeah. I get it. Go kill it at the shoot."

Journee grabs her keys and heads out. As soon as she's gone, I text the guys to finalize our plans. Man, I need this. With all our practices and shows . . . I just need to drink and get high.

I straighten up my apartment a bit before settling on the couch to watch a football game, waiting for them to come over. The game's just about to end when there's a knock on the door.

"Hey, Knox. I hope you don't mind us bringing a few friends with us," Reid says as he comes in, Ezra and three girls I don't know trailing behind him.

Ezra gestures toward the girls, who are each taking a seat on my couch. "This is Delaney, Quinn, and Rory."

"Nice apartment," the one named Quinn says.

"Thank you," I say as I get up to grab some beers from the fridge.

"Do you live alone?" one of the others asks. I think it's Delaney?

I hand her a beer. "My girlfriend lives with me."

"Oh, too bad. You're cute."

Quinn leans closer to Delaney, but I can hear her loud and clear. "I bet you can get him to fuck you by the end of the night with no problem, Laney."

"Quinn, he has a girlfriend," Ezra cuts in. I *do* have a girlfriend. Last time I checked, they do too. But I guess they don't give a fuck about Sarai or Willow right now.

Rory takes a swig of beer. "So?"

I don't know what these guys were thinking, bringing these girls over to my apartment, so I just focus on drinking my beer. Laney is super hot . . . but I have Journee. Damn, it is tempting though.

We mingle a bit, talking about whatever, before we bring out the weed. I go a little overboard, smoking four joints and chugging two more beers on top of that.

I'm more than buzzed and more than a little high. Is the room spinning a bit? Next thing I know, a chick comes over and starts to making out with me. Laney, right? This is Laney. Yeah.

As Laney and I are making out, I feel her slip something into my pants pocket. Damn. Where are Reid and Ezra? Oh, they're making out with the other chicks. Fuck them. They got girlfriends too, but they were so ready to point out I have one.

I'm disoriented as fuck, so I really don't know what's going on. The next thing I know, I'm stark naked on my bed with whoever this chick is that Ezra and Reid brought over on top of me fucking the shit out of me.

After it's all said and done, this chick just up and leaves. I lie on my bed alone to try and process what just happened. This was supposed to have been a guys get-together. I wasn't expecting them to bring girls over. Guilt starts to creep in, then depression, then anger. What the fuck did I just do?

My emotions get the best of me, and I'm like "Fuck it." I go back into the kitchen and grab two more beers. I drink them straight down. Then I roll a few more joints and smoke them as well. I'm so angry at myself for letting this happen. I'm also angry at Journee for not being here when clearly I needed her to be.

SIX

Journee

We took photos during the daylight and at sunset. Todd Werner loved the shots he took of me, and I was so thrilled he let me preview the pictures through his camera lens.

I text Knox to let him know I'm on my way home, but I don't get a response the whole ride, which is weird. It's not like him to not respond. It's pitch black when I make it inside the apartment. There isn't one light on, and the place reeks of weed and alcohol. I look around, and the apartment is literally trashed.

"Knox? Knox!" No answer.

My heart starts to race and pound out of my chest. What if something terrible happened while I was gone? Nervous, I approach our bedroom. What if Knox is passed out on the floor? Or worse . . . No, I don't want to think about that.

I go inside our bedroom only to let out a scream when Knox grabs me by my arms and starts ripping my clothes off. He digs his nails deep into my skin, causing me to whimper in pain at how aggressive he is. Then he throws me onto our bed. The sheets feel like sand paper on my exposed body, gritty and abrasive. As I'm lying on the bed, Knox slides my panties down my legs and hurls them to the floor. He undoes his zipper and pulls out his dick. He climbs on top of me and tightly holds my wrists right above my head. Knox parts my legs with his knee. He shoves his dick deep inside me and starts thrusting back and forth.

"I waited forever to fuck your brains out," he whispers, as if enjoying my pain.

He continues thrusting in and out, deep and hard, and I don't know what to think. He's never acted like this before. This is the first time he's fucked me without a condom on, and it hurts. It feels like he's ripping my insides out. He's huge, and every thrust makes my eyes water —it's so painful. Seeing the expression on my face, Knox speeds up his rhythm and tells me he *wants* to make me bleed, *wants* to make me sore.

"You are mine, and I can do whatever the hell I want to you," he says in cruel delight.

"Your daddy can't save you now. You are my little whore."

After what seems like an eternity, Knox finally pulls out. But he isn't through with me yet. He cups my jaw with his rough, calloused fingers. I clench my mouth shut, realizing what he wants me to do. This makes him even angrier. His grip tightens, forcing my mouth open, and he forces the tip of his dick right between my lips. All I can taste is his salty semen as he begins moving his dick around in my mouth.

"Suck it, like a straw, baby," he all but demands.

"You know you want to." I do as I'm told, and I sit there until my mouth is filled with his semen. Knox pulls out and holds my jaws closed. "Now swallow it."

I do.

He smirks. "Good girl." He then gets up and steps back into his boxers, which had previously been discarded on the floor. I can only lie there, stark naked, sore, and bleeding—like he promised. "Don't bother getting dressed," he says before he leaves for the living room. "I'll be back for more."

Once he's gone, I'm free to wonder what in the hell is happening. Why is he like this? How did he get to this point? The covers on the bed are all disheveled, and I can see where my blood has stained the sheets. I'm afraid to move because of the pain. My throat feels like it's on fire, and all I want is a drink to quench the burning sensation. I can hear Knox in the kitchen opening the fridge—probably to grab a beer—before turning on the TV.

After a while, Knox comes back into the bedroom, and he has a friend with him.

"Journee, Laney. Laney, Journee," he introduces us, a devilish look in his eyes

I'm still naked, but I'm under the covers at this point. Knox doesn't seem to care. "Get up and come here," he commands. I get up and stand right next to him, trying to control my slight muscle spasms.

Then he says, "Kiss her."

I blink. "What?"

"I say kiss her." He raises his voice ever so slightly. "Now!"

Laney is just standing there. I hesitate at first, but seeing how Knox is in rare form tonight, I don't disobey. She kisses me back, tongue and all. Knox watches us, his dick out, pumping himself, and I can't help but wonder what he'll have us do next.

After Laney and I finish making out, Knox turns to her. "Strip." Laney starts taking her clothes off, and then we're both naked in front of him.

Knox smirks. "Bend over, ladies. I'm going to enjoy fucking both of you in the ass." Laney and I both do what he says. We bend over, with our hands on the edge of the bed and asses in the air.

"You're first, my little whore," he tells me.

His dick sprung straight in the air, he lowers himself and slowly pushes it in my ass. No lubrication, no prep—it hurts like hell. Which is probably exactly what he wants. The rapid in-and-out motion of his dick burns. My body goes in sync with the movement of it. He moves to Laney after a while and fucks her in the ass too.

When he's done, he says, "There's one more thing I would like to witness."

"What's that?" I say, Laney and I both still bent over.

"Laney, lay on the bed and spread your legs," he orders her. She does exactly what Knox says. "Journee, eat her out," he instructs.

"Hell no," I tell him. That earns me a forceful slap across the face.

"I said go down on her," Knox says, voice raised as he pushes me toward her pussy.

"Now, do it."

Laney lets out several breathy moans as I go down on her. Her whole body jerks, and she starts grinding her hips wildly. Then Laney finally climaxes and comes in my mouth with Knox just standing there and watching us with a sinister grin. He yanks me by the hair and pulls me away from Laney before telling her to get dressed and leave. I start crying when she's gone, and my gag reflexes kick in as I try throwing up Laney's cum. My mind is completely fucked as to why Knox had me do these things. He's either not himself, just wanted to get his kicks off, or both.

As I'm bawling, curled up on the floor, Knox sits right beside me. "I wanted to break your spirit so much that reliving the pain I just inflicted on you was your only option." He places my hands on his dick. "I'm sore. Can you rub it for me?"

I dare not tell him no after what he just made me do. So I massage his dick. "Yes, baby. Harder. Fuck, yes," he moans, bucking his hips into my hands. It isn't long before he comes, and makes me lick the mess off my hands. He kisses me after.

"Thanks, babe." He picks me up, lays me on the bed, and puts the covers on me. "Now get some sleep," he says nonchalantly, as if this whole night never happened.

The dream starts with me standing in the middle of a lit room. Then the room goes dark. Shards of glass start falling from the ceiling and scrape up my skin. I wake up from this dream with my heart pounding out of my chest, sweating profusely. I remember feeling like I needed to see the blood from the glass cutting my skin, as if it were the only way I could feel alive. It's a hard pill to swallow—knowing that I put myself in this situation. I thought I knew Knox. I thought he wouldn't dare hurt me. I gave up the opportunity to go move with my dad to live with Knox. I trusted him. My dad trusted him, and this is what the fucking bastard does. I start shaking because I'm so angry. I want to throw something, anything. But instead, I just bawl my eyes out for what feels like the millionth time this morning.

I get a voicemail message from a photographer who wants to confirm if I am still available this afternoon for an ad shoot for Camp Out, a local campsite. They want to draw in more college-age people. He also asks if I got the outfit he chose for me from The Casual Corner, a clothing store. The campsite isn't actually that far away, meaning I don't have to drive two hours away again. I'm thankful for that, but how the fuck am I going to do a photoshoot and have people touch me without wanting to spazz out on them? Breathe. I decide the hell with it. I need the money, and I need to build my portfolio.

I make my way to the bathroom. I'm sore all over, and it really hurts to walk, but I manage. I don't feel like taking a shower, so I run a bath instead. I let the water fill up the tub to the brim. I'm not really paying that much attention and almost let the water overflow. I look at myself in the mirror before I get in. That is the biggest mistake. I don't see myself. Instead, I see all the bruises—on my face, down my neck, on my wrists where Knox squeezed my arms together above my head. I don't even want to look at the rest of my body, so I turn away and step into the tub.

I submerge myself in the lukewarm water. While

I'm under the water, my thoughts drift to a dangerous place. I could easily let myself drown, and Knox could totally be blamed for my death. Ha! That would be shitty for him. But then I think about my dad. He would have to also deal with my death on top of my mom's, which would be unfair to him. I wouldn't want to subject him to more pain, even more than what he's already been through. While I'm so tempted let myself drown, I finally come up for air.

I dry off, then go back into my bedroom to get dressed. This photoshoot, I was told, will take place at a hiking trail in the woods. I'm about to open the package I ordered per the photographer's suggestion, and I am nervous. The outfit is a knee-length, Aztec-print dress and brown knee-high boots. The dress sports red, brown, blue, white, black, and gray patterns. It's so cute, and it fits perfectly. I look through the package for the gold earrings and brown fringe belt that go with it. I'm so excited, though I am a little apprehensive too. I'm worried about all that transpired with me over the course of the morning. But I'm not going to let that stop me from pursuing my dreams.

I drive to the hiking trail we're using for the shoot. The drive up is a cathartic release I very much needed. The scenery is breathtaking. The trees are tall, with their colorful leaves blowing in the wind. Such beauty, even in the eyes of a broken girl. It, oddly enough, reminds me of the first date Knox and I went on at the botanical garden. I've been crying off and on the whole morning, and this is what I needed to feel grounded again. I'm not sure how things will go with my emotional state, but this is what I love to do, and nothing will put a damper on my ambition.

As soon as I arrive at the hiking trail, I park my car, but sit in it for a few minutes to collect my thoughts before going into the photoshoot. I don't want the photographer to sense something's wrong. I am not ready to tell to anyone that I've been raped by my boyfriend. That's why I put on a layer of makeup prior. I don't want anyone to see the bruises on my face or my body. Thank God for concealer. I finally get the courage to get out of my car and walk up to the trail.

Connor Abrams is a local photographer. He's forty-two years old, with salt and pepper hair, and is dressed in slacks and a button-down shirt—very dapper looking. He has about five people on his crew. There's also another model that's at the shoot. She looks about my age, with long black hair and green eyes, and she is wearing a similar-looking Aztec-print dress with kneehigh boots.

"Journee, so glad you could come to this shoot," Connor tells me as I'm walking up to where they are.

"Thank you for this opportunity, Mr. Abrams."

"Call me Connor, Journee. This is Francesca. She will be taking part in the shoot as well."

"Hey, Francesca," I say, extending my hand. "It's nice to meet you."

"Call me Chesca. And we do hugs around here," Chesca states as she embraces me.

I don't know how I feel during or after her embrace. It's weird. I don't think I feel anything, to be honest. I just feel hollow and numb. I know I'm somewhat rigid, but at least I don't pull away from her.

"Journee, you're up first," Connor says. I listen to how and where he wants me to pose. First up is hugging a nearby tree with one knee bent. An easy enough pose. I smile at Connor's lens, and the flashes of the camera take over.

"Great, Journee. You look like a natural. But wait— your hair." Conner starts walking toward me. I hold my breath as he fixes my hair. He then gives me a puzzled look. Did I flinch when he touched me?

"I'm okay," I tell him.

"Are you sure?"

I give him a half-smile. "Yes."

Shit. I don't want to give off the vibe that something's wrong with me, but that quickly fails. Now I have Francesca looking at me, as well as the bluish-green-eyed guy that's also on the crew. Damn it.

"Why don't we let Chesca go," Connor says. "We'll give you a little break, okay, Journee?"

I step away from the tree to go sit in a one of those portable fold-up chairs. I sit there, watching how effortlessly Chesca works the camera. She"s definitely a natural, and I can"t help but wonder if she has any dark secrets too. Has she dealt with what I went through? Does she have some hidden trauma too?

"Yes, Chesca. Good, good," Connor says between flashes.

Out of the corner of my eye, I feel the guy from earlier glancing at me. He acts like he can't take his eyes off of me. What is he staring at? I'm tempted throw a mean glare back at him, but I don't want to make a scene or have him think I'm a bitch. So I just keep watching Chesca.

Finishing up, Conner politely asks me, "Would you like to try again, Journee?"

"Can we just call it a day? I'm sorry. It's my fault. I shouldn't have committed to this if I wasn't up to it," I tell him honestly.

"Yes, sure. Don't apologize. There will be other photoshoots in the future. I will definitely keep you in mind."

"Thank you for understanding."

Connor invites us all to have lunch at Curry Collective, a local Thai restaurant. Before we head to the restaurant, while I'm about to walk to my car, Chesca stops me. "Hey, I noticed how fidgety you were back there. Was this your first photoshoot?"

"No, it's not. I just went through something this morning," I tell her vaguely.

"Oh . . ." She looks concerned.

"Let's go, girls," Connor calls out to us from his car.

"I'm okay," I say to Chesca, getting into my car. "I'll see you at the restaurant."

Connor, Chesca, and the rest of the crew beat me to Curry Collective. So I quickly park my car and grab my cell and purse before heading into the restaurant. I glance down at my cell. Knox never even texted me. I could have been dead in a ditch somewhere. Would he even give two fucks about it? Even though what happened this morning was traumatizing, part of me wants Knox to own up to what he did. As sick as this sounds, after all

I've been through, I still love him.

"We have eight people," Connor says as a one of the workers, a woman, comes up to the front stand.

"Right this way." She leads us to a private room in the back. As we sit around the table, she's hands us the menus. "I'll give you a few minutes to look over the menus. I'll go and get us some waters."

"So are you sure you're okay, Journee?" Connor asks me as we wait, some of the others already browsing the food selection.

"Yes, I'm fine." I don't want to get into the reason why I had a slight spasm attack earlier.

Certainly not with Connor Abrams, nor anyone else sitting at the table.

"I'm glad you're okay."

The waitress comes with our waters and takes all of our orders. We all start talking after she leaves, mainly about modeling and photography. I tell them about how I came to want to be a model, and the infamous story of the photoshoot I walked off of. All the while I'm talking, the guy with the bluish-green eyes is yet again staring me down.

"Can I be excused for a minute?" I say when I'm done. I need to get away from his prying eyes.

I get up from the table and walk out the door. Fresh air. That's what I need. I sit on the bench in front of the restaurant and take a few deep breaths in, exhaling out slowly. I check my cell to see if I missed a text from Knox. Nope.

"Hey, do you mind if I sit?" a voice that I was unfamiliar with says.

I look up, and it sure enough is that guy. What the hell does he want?

"Sure," I say hesitantly.

He takes a seat next to me and doesn't waste any time interrogating me. "I'm no expert, but I can tell when someone is lying."

"Lying? About what?"

"I can see your bruises from a mile away," he says matter-of-factly.

"Oh, really?" I say, annoyed.

"I was just saying."

"What are you trying to prove?"

"Nothing. I'm not trying to prove anything . . . Just that you don't deserve this. Whoever did this to you is an asshole."

"Maybe he's not an asshole," I say, defending Knox. "Maybe he just made a mistake, had a lapse in judgment."

I'm totally fed up at this point. How dare he? What right does this guy have to talk to me about my boyfriend and how he treats me? I want to tell this guy to fuck off . . . But that would probably not be the best idea. Man, I really don't want to go back inside knowing he—whatever the hell his name is—is going to be there.

Curiosity gets the better of me, despite how livid I am. "What's your name, by the way?"

"I'm just an intern, so that is all you need to know me as," he states. I roll my eyes at him, and he laughs. He really is starting to piss me off.

"Connor just texted me the food is here.

Shall we go back inside?" he asks

I don't answer him, choosing to go back to the table and start eating. Chesca looks at me, puzzled, as I give the intern dagger eyes. After I finished eating, I tell the group that I have to leave, and they all thank me for coming.

Connor stops me before I get to the door. "I have another shoot coming up, and I would love to have you in it."

"I would love to."

"Great! I will email you all the details later," he states.

I'm so excited that Connor doesn't hold what happened at today's shoot against me and has decided to give me another chance. I confidently walk out of the restaurant only to glance back and see the intern still looking at me, but this time concerned. I just brush it off and keep walking to my car. The nerve of him. He doesn't know my situation. It's none of his business anyway. I don't know why I even talked to him. Such a waste of my time. Knox isn't that bad— no different from any other guy. Fuck it. Let me just go home.

ILLICIT DOSE OF SCARS

SEVEN

Knox

Ezra, Reid, and I call a songwriting session to formulate some new songs for a gig we have coming up.

"Where's Journee?" Ezra asks after a while.

"I don't really know. She hasn't texted me all day," I say.

"Did something happen between you two?" Reid interjects.

I go quiet as I try to remember what happened last night. I was upset because Laney got me to fuck her. That I do remember. I wanted revenge on that manipulative bitch. But I was also mad at Journee in the back of my mind. She wasn't there for me when I needed her. So when she finally came home, I ended up taking my frustration out on her too. The whole situation was fucked up, and now I don"t know how to fix it.

"No, nothing happened between us," I lie.

We continue working on lyrics for some of our new songs. Then Journee comes through the front door and hurries into our bedroom. I want to check on her, so

I ask the guys to wait.

They both nod and resume writing while I rush into the bedroom and shut the door

"Journee," I begin.

"What! What do you want, Knox?" she says, coming over and pinning me against the wall. She kneels in front of me and starts undoing my belt buckle. My pants and boxers come down. There's this desperate look in her eyes as she takes my cock in her mouth.

"Shit . . . Journee." I let out a moan and claw the wall with my fingers as she begins roughly sucking on my cock, which is quickly growing hard.

She pulls it out of her mouth for a brief second. "This is what you wanted. Right? Well, instead of forcing me, I'm giving it to you."

She doesn't stop until I come in her mouth, and I don't know what to think. I feel like shit; I don't even really remember what I did to her. But I feel like a total asshole, knowing that she was just giving me head so, in her words, "I wouldn't have to force her again."

Journee goes into our bathroom and starts crying. She doesn't lock the door, so I go in the bathroom and embrace her. She tries pulling away, but I don't let her.

"Listen, I'm so sorry about what I did," I say. Journee just starts crying even harder into my shirt. "Babe, I wasn't myself," I insist. "I was high and drunk. I barely even remember half of what I did or made you do."

"Fuck you for not remembering," she says, pulling away from me angrily. "I just came from a photoshoot I couldn't do because I wasn't fully there."

"I don't know what you want me to say, honestly,"
"Just forget it. I guess I'm just your little whore."
"What?" I say, puzzled.

She leaves our bathroom, climbs into our bed, and buries herself under the covers. I decide to leave her alone for now, so I go back out into the living room, where Ezra and Reid are talking.

Ezra is the first to notice me. "Is everything okay?"

"Yeah, you were in there for a minute," Reid says.
"Everything is okay . . . I guess," I tell them.

"What happened?" Ezra asks. "You don't look like everything's going to be okay."

"I don't want to talk about it. Can you guys just leave?" I say as I rake my hand through my hair. "I'm sorry. I'm fucked right now, and I can't deal."

As soon as they leave, I go back into our bedroom and climb into the bed next to Journee. It's clear she doesn't want to have anything to do with me at this moment. But her angry fit just a second ago turned me on so bad. I climb on top of her and pin her to the bed. She doesn't try to get away from me.

I whisper in her ear. "I'm sorry, but I want you. You are sexy, and you are mine. I will be gentle this time."

Her breathing starts to calm as I kiss her. She kisses me back. I undress her and trail my fingers along her naked body. She lets out a series of moans before I enter her. Journee digs her nails into my back, scratching the hell out it. But the pain, mixed with pleasure, is something I didn't mind.

"You didn't have to give me head earlier, but I

enjoyed every minute of it," I tell her. "So I want to return the favor. Is that okay?"

"Okay," Journee says as she braces herself.

I roll back the covers and position myself between her legs, propping them over my shoulders. I lick her slit and pay extra attention to her clit, sucking it every once in a while. Journee arches her body, her toes curled, as I continue. She lets out a scream of pleasure before she comes, and I lap up every last drop.

"Oh my god," she moans.

I smirk up at her. "I'm glad I could be of service to you."

I lie next to her as she stares at the ceiling with glassy eyes. What is she thinking? She was compliant this time, or was it all a front? I so desperately want to get into her head right now. The one thing I learned about Journee since we've started dating is she internalizes how she really feels. It takes a while for her to warm up to a person. I don't even know some of the deep, painful things she's been through, other than her mother's death. I know her mother passed away from liver cancer, but that's all Journee would say. She didn't go into detail. It was not that she didn't want me to know. She just couldn't bring herself to come to terms with it. So she felt better not saying much at all.

"Journee . . .what's wrong?" I finally ask her

"Nothing. I guess we're even now, right? I gave you want you wanted. You gave me what you *thought* I wanted."

"You didn't want me to do that to you?"

"You own me, remember? You said you wanted to

break my spirit so much that my only option was to find relief from the pain. Well, lucky you. You succeeded."

Tears stream down her face, and I don't have the right words to convey to her. So I just move to the living room and lie on the couch. Thoughts haunt my mind as I try closing my eyes to go to sleep. Everything is still fuzzy from that night, but whatever I did, it was terrible.

Disco Ball, a local dance club, is having a grand opening, and Hendrix Schulz, the club manager, wants us to make an appearance and play a few songs. Now that we've played a few arena shows these past few months, we're stoked to play a more intimate crowd.

"Are you almost ready, babe?" I ask Journee, putting on my combat boots.

"Almost," Journee answers as she's fixing her hair in our dresser mirror.

She's wearing a black tank top under my oversized red-and-black plaid button-down, a black belt around her waist. Skinny jeans hug her legs, as do the black boots that go up past her knees.

I stare her down. "Anything you wear always puts me in the mood to jump you."

"Calm down," she says, laughing. "You have a performance to get to."

It took her a while to get to this point, to trust me again. I know I fucked up big time, and while I can't promise her that I won't fuck up again, to have my girlfriend back and present with me is something I don't and won't take lightly.

On the drive to the club, Journee and I reminisce about how we met.

"What made you build up the courage to call me?" I ask her.

"At first I didn't know what your intentions were, or why in the world you put your cell number, but then I thought, 'That was a smooth move on his part.' So I decided to take the chance," she explains.

"Oh . . . you thought I was a man whore who wants to fuck all the women I meet at my concerts. You can be honest, Jour, if that's what you thought."

"Sort of . . . But then I got to know you, and you aren't like that at all."

"Well I appreciate you giving me a chance to prove myself," I say.

"What made you decide to give me your number anyway?"

"I thought you were so damn cute, and I wanted a chance to play in those curls of yours,"

She cocks her head to the side. "So your intentions *were* to try to fuck me."

"Well . . . not at first," I say slyly.

Journee rolls her eyes.

We pull up to the club, and there's a long line to get inside. Journee and I wait in the parking lot until we see Ezra and Reid pull up. Our manager, Seth, told us we would be let in through the back door, so we all head to the back and knock.

Hendrix opens the door. "Come on in and set up."

The guys and I decide to get a feel for stage before we set up. It's a decent size, not too big or small. Standing on it, we have an excellent view of the entire room. Satisfied, we go back out to our cars and haul our instruments and other equipment inside. Some of the club staff offer to help us too.

Journee stays inside the club and watches us set up. "This looks kick-ass."

"Thanks, babe," I call back as we continue setting up.

Before they let the crowd in, the staff brings over some food they ordered specially for us. We eat and talk, gearing up for the show. Journee gives us a little pep talk before we take the stage. I love the fucking hell out of this girl. She definitely knows how to pump us up as a band, and certainly me as her boyfriend. I could have a million fan girls wanting and lusting after me, but the only girl I see and want in my bed is Journee.

We play five of our older songs, then the four new songs off of our new EP, before rounding it off with a new song we started working on the last few practices. Overall, the performance is a success, and we are pretty sure we have gained a bunch of new fans tonight.

"Want to dance?" Journee asks me when the band is finished with our set.

I kiss her. "Of course, beautiful."

We start dancing, and she, in typical Journee fashion, takes my breath away. She starts grinding on me, which sends jolts straight to my cock. It's so tempting to want to take her right in the middle of this dance floor.

Someone taps me on the shoulder. "Hey, could

you come here for a second?" Ezra says, a concerned look on his face.

I pull away from Journee, who now shares Ezra's concerned look. "It's okay, Journee. I'll be right back," I tell her, trying to ease her worry before following Ezra out to a private part of the club.

"What's up?" I ask.

"The past coming back to haunt us," he mutters.

"I don't quite understand."

"Just come on, and keep walking."

When we get there, I see two girls looking very upset while talking with Reid. As Ezra and I approach, they both go quiet and glare at me, their arms folded against their chests.

"What up, ladies," I say to break the clear tension.

"I don't know if you remember us from your little get-together a while back," one of them says.

"What?" I say, puzzled.

"This is Rory and Quinn, from the night we had our little party," Reid states.

"Oh . . . hi," I say nonchalantly.

"You may want to listen to them, Knox," Reid says sternly, "because from what they've disclosed to me—"

"What actually happened *that* night?" one of the girls cuts in. Quinn, was it?

"Weren't you there? You *know* what happened that night," I tell her.

"Did you sleep with Laney?"

"Yeah, but I wasn't all there, and she knew it," I tell them straight up.

"That's not what we heard. Laney told us that you called her back over after we all left and ass-fucked her and made your girlfriend go down on her."

"I don't know what the hell you are talking about. Laney forced me to have sex with her, knowing I was crossed as fuck. After that, I don't remember at all what happened."

"You're a fucking liar, and you better watch your back," the other girl—must be Rory— threatens, then walks out of the club with Quinn.

"What the fuck was that all about?" I shake my head, still shocked and puzzled.

"Listen," Reid says. "I don't know what happened that night. But we definitely have to watch who we bring to our get-togethers."

Just then, Journee comes out to where we are. "Hey, guys. I've been looking all over for you." Noticing the expressions on our faces, she adds, "What's wrong?"

"It's nothing. Just a few jealous fans. That's all," I quickly tell her.

The threat from Rory doesn't leave my mind. It actually takes me back to the reason I started playing the guitar in the first place.

I was a freshman in high school, with a police officer for a dad. My mom worked as a receptionist at a health clinic. The house I grew up in was a two-story house with four rooms. The two extra rooms were used as offices—one for my mom and one for my dad. Since I was the only child, I got spoiled a lot.

We lived in a rough part of town, but despite this, they wanted me to have a happy, wholesome childhood.

And for the most part it was, until I got to high school and the bullying began. I was a quiet and reserved kid. I got good grades, and most of my teachers actually liked me. I guess Rush Cantor noticed that, and it was enough for him to want to mess with me.

I remember when the bullying got too much for me to handle, and I just snapped. My grades were falling, and I had withdrawn into myself more than usual. My parents were at their wits' ends. I was getting my ass kicked almost every other day, and I had to take matters in my own hands.

It was a Monday morning, and my mom and dad were still sleeping. I got up and rummaged through my father's office to find his extra gun. He had bought it for my mom in case of emergencies, when he wasn't there. I put the gun in my book bag. It was the last straw. I wanted to kill Rush, to rid him of his very existence.

After grabbing breakfast to go, I walked to school like I did every morning, since it was so close to home. There were metal detectors at the entrance of the high school, so I texted one of my classmates to let me in through a side door. Once inside, I walked to my classes with ease. It wasn't until math class that I had any trouble with Rush. Sitting in a desk across from me, he started taunting me when the teacher stepped out of the room. I told him to stop, glancing around at my classmates who decided that they were going to join in.

"What are you going to do?" he hissed.

That's when I grabbed the gun from my backpack. I got up from my desk and, standing behind him, put the gun to his temple. "Blow your fucking brains out," I threatened him.

By then, everyone realized I wasn't joking. A few students muttered some curses before running out. Rush started sweating and pleaded with me not to kill him.

I held the gun securely to Rush's head, all set to pull the trigger. "Why the hell shouldn't I? You've been tormenting me since my first day."

Everything was a blur after that. Someone tackled me to the ground and knocked the gun from my hands. I was handcuffed and escorted outside, into a police car. They questioned me and gave me a mental evaluation at the station before calling my parents. My father was pissed. He was reprimanded by the chief of police and was almost let go because I was a dumbass.

After the school incident, my mother had to quit her job at the health clinic. It was the last thing she wanted to do, but no other school wanted to enroll me. They thought I was a potential threat. So my mom ended up homeschooling me for the entire three and a half years I had left of high school.

I was ordered to go to therapy, which lasted a good six months. I quit going after that, telling my dad I wanted to learn to play the guitar, in love with the sound after listening to a lot of heavy metal and both alternative and classic rock. My dad agreed to buy me my first electric guitar, which was stained black and silver.

I learned the guitar rather quickly. I became obsessed with it and started writing my own song lyrics because I got tired of playing songs by other artists. It wasn't long till I started dreaming of the day that I could start my own band. I already knew what I wanted to call us: Supposed Posers.

After I finished my high school studies, I had no desire to go to college. I just wanted to start a band. So I made an ad on my laptop: "Eighteen-year-old guitarist is looking for a lead singer and a drummer to start a rock band." I posted it everywhere on social media. After getting a few guys who didn't wanted to commit wholeheartedly, I got depressed.

"Don't give up," my mom said every time I got down. "You are an excellent guitarist. It'll happen for you in due time."

One day, it finally did. I got two responses to my ad, one from a singer named Ezra, who, in his words, wanted to a chance to scream his pain and anger through the many songs he'd written over the years. My kind of guy. The other was from a drummer named Reid, who had been playing the drums since he was eight years old. They both were nineteen years old, and they both wrote they wanted an opportunity to showcase their talents to the world. I quickly emailed them back; I wanted to meet them. It only took one meeting and practice to know we had something special.

EIGHT

Journee

"How long will you be gone for?" I ask Knox as he's packing his suitcase.

"Three weeks," he replies. "Will you be okay? I'm going to miss you terribly."

"I'll be fine. My dad just texted me now, asking me if he could visit," I explain.

"Perfect. Ask him if he could stay for a week or two so you won't have to be alone the entire time I'm away."

"That's a good idea. Maybe I can convince him to stay a week."

Knox continues packing his suitcase, and wishes I were going with him. I've been to several of their local shows, but never one in a different state. I know all the shows are somewhat similar, but this is the first time I'll be away from him for a long period of time.

"Babe, don't go. I'm going to miss you," I pout.

Knox stops packing and comes over to the bed. "You know I hate leaving you like this, but my job calls. Three weeks away without your pussy is going to fucking kill me. But I'll manage somehow." He gives me a long lingering look.

"Oh, really? How much time do we have before you have to go?" I ask him playfully.

He smirked. "About half an hour."

"Well, then . . ." I pull him close and kiss him.

He kisses me back like it'll be the last time we'll have sex. It technically *will* be, for three weeks. Besides, he isn't the only one feeling horny at this moment. But then my phone starts to vibrate, totally killing the mood.

"Shit! I think it's my dad." I squirm away from Knox.

"Damn, Journee. Way to kill the vibe," Knox says after I grab my phone.

"Sorry, babe," I say, reading the message from my dad. "You have to leave soon anyway."

Knox looks down at my cell to check the time. "Yeah. I do."

He gets dressed and packs the last of his things. He comes over and gives me a lingering goodbye kiss. "I love you so much. I'll text you when we get there."

As soon as Knox is gone, I text my dad back.

Knox is going out of town for a gig. He'll be gone for three weeks.

Dad: *Oh really! Tell him I said have a great mini tour.*

I know you wanted to visit. Maybe you can stay for a week? I'm going to be here alone, and it would be good to have your company. I miss and love you.

Dad: *Of course I'd be up to staying with you for a week. I just have to get the okay to take off from my job since it's so soon. So I'll get back to you, okay? I miss you too, baby girl.*

It'll be really great to see my dad. I haven't seen him since he left, though I'd understand if he can't, since he's still considered pretty new at his job.

I decide to search for more modeling gigs just in case my dad can't come to visit. That way I wouldn't have to sit in the apartment, twiddling my thumbs, waiting for Knox to return. It's like I really don't have any friends here. After high school all my friends moved or went away for college. I opted not to go to college. It wasn't for me. I hated sitting in class in high school, and I knew college wouldn't be any different. Besides, I was always into the fashion industry, intrigued by the lives of models. One day, it clicked for me that that's what I wanted to do. I'm still just starting my modeling career, so I have a lot to learn still, but I don't want to do anything else.

While I was surfing the internet for modeling gigs, my cell vibrates.

Knox: *Hey, Jour, we made it here safely. Checking into the hotel now. Is your dad coming to visit?*

Glad you guys made it safely. Still waiting on my dad to text me back that his job let him take off.

Knox: *Our first show is tomorrow night, so we are just going to explore the city today.*

We might go get some drinks later on though
Good luck on your show tomorrow night. I know you guys will rock it! Be safe, and don't drink too much.

Knox: *I'll miss you and your beautiful face, but I will see you in three weeks and we'll make up for the time apart!*

I continue looking for modeling gigs, but I hope my dad texts soon. I want to know as soon as possible if I can book something for the week he might come, or if I need to wait till after. Luckily, just as I decide to call it quits for the day, my phone vibrates, flashing my dad's name.

Dad: *Great news Jour, I'm able to take a week off from my job. How about I come next week?*

Next week is perfect. I can't wait to see you.

I'm so happy. I miss him terribly and really want him to visit me. But now I have a lot to do before next week. I want get groceries so we don't have to spend money eating out. I've gotten a little better at cooking. Knox seems to enjoy the dishes I make, and I'm confident that my dad will noticed the improvement in my cooking skills as well.

This apartment is a mess though. So I really have

to clean it up. I'm not naive to hope my dad doesn't know that Knox and I have sex, but Knox keeps his condoms on the nightstand next to our bed. Those definitely need to be put in the drawers before my dad spots them. I plan to give him an apartment tour, and it's little things like that I have to remember. But I'm super excited to see my dad and find out what's new with him.

I haul ass and finish wiping down the counters and text Knox to let him know about a photoshoot I booked. I quickly throw on some sweats and head out the door.

According to my GPS, it would only take ten minutes to arrive at Connor's studio. I didn't know it was so close to my apartment. While on the short drive there, I think about my last photoshoot with Connor and how I spazzed out on him. I pray that this shoot won't affect me like the last time. I don't want to be haunted by the "incident" forever. I don't want it to ruin my chances of ever getting a modeling contract, and I definitely don't want it to prevent me from wanting to model at all. But it's a part of me that I have to deal with, like a sore that won't heal even after it's scabbed over.

I walk into Connor's studio, determined to kick ass. I really want to prove to him that what happened at the last photoshoot won't happen again. That I'm confident and secure in myself.

"Journee, perfect timing," Connor says when I walk into his studio. "Let's get you into hair and makeup and find you an outfit to wear."

I normally don't wear a lot of makeup. Knox prefers the natural look on me. He said he was accustomed to his exes wearing a shitload of makeup, and when he wanted to see them bare faced, they weren't comfortable showing him. He didn't fault them for that, but he soon realized they always wanted to look perfect and put together because of who he was. When I came along, he said it was refreshing to see a woman who was comfortable in her own skin. So the only times I wear a lot of makeup are for photoshoots and when Knox and I are going to a special event.

After I'm done with hair and makeup, they give me an outfit to wear for the shoot.

Connor calls me over afterward to meet who I'm doing the photoshoot with.

"This is Jett. He's been in several magazines, as well as in a few movies."

Jett is at least six foot five, is muscular, and has hazel eyes and olive skin. He is gorgeous, almost making me forget I have a boyfriend. Oops.

I extend my hand for a handshake. "Hey, I'm Journee. It's nice to meet you."

"It's nice to meet you too," Jett says in what seems to be a heavy Greek accent as he shakes my hand.

Even his touch is soft and inviting. Jett and I take our positions in front of a white background. First, we act as if we are flirting from afar. Connor snaps a handful of photos and tells us that they will go inside the magazine. They apparently want to interview us to talk about our modeling journeys. This be my first interview ever with a magazine, and I'm super excited and nervous at the same time.

We take a short break before Connor shoots for the cover photo, so I sit and chat with Jett. He tells me he grew up in Greece with his brother and two sisters. Jett moved to the states to live with his aunt after he finished his secondary education. He was discovered while walking through the mall, and the rest was history. It's fascinating to hear the story of how he became a model. In return, I tell him how I grew up loving fashion, and wanted to be a part of the fashion industry for as long as I can remember.

"You guys ready?" Connor cuts in.

Jett and I get back in our places while Connor gives us our next pose, which is Jett holding me by the waist and looking deep into my eyes.

I tell myself not to lose my shit as I take a few deep breaths. I look Jett in the eyes, trying to hide my pain. They're so beautiful, so soft and understanding. Connor takes a few pictures of us embracing. Then Jett slips his hands underneath my top slightly, exposing a little of my bare skin and totally freaking me out. Connor seems to like it, maybe thinking it fits the mood of our pose.

"Great. This is good. Perfect," Connor says, still snapping photos. "You two have amazing chemistry."

I looked into Jett's hazel eyes, trying to focus on how warm and stunningly beautiful they are, but I can feel myself trying to hold back my tears. I give Jett a strained smile as his eyes search mine, as if he's looking for a secret buried underneath the scars on my heart.

I pull away from Jett. "Fuck."

"Wait. What?" I can hear the confusion in Connor's voice as I retreat to the bathroom.

I throw water on my face, feeling like shit because

I'm basically fucking up my modeling career thanks to what Knox did. Why am I giving him so much power—well not him, more so the "incident." Maybe I should talk to someone. But I don't want anyone in my business. I don't want them saying I should leave my boyfriend when he hasn't done anything else like that to me.

It was just that one time, that one lapse in judgement.

Someone knocks on the bathroom door. "Journee? Are you okay?" Connor asks, concerned.

Startled, I hesitantly reply back, "Yes, I'm fine." I finally open the door and walk past Connor. I go back into the main part of the studio and sit down.

"Journee, did I do something wrong?" Jett says, walking over.

"No. You were nothing but patient and a wonderful delight to work with. It's me."

"You were really tense as I was holding you, and then you ran into the bathroom. I thought—"

I cut him off and look into his eyes with sincerity. "You did nothing wrong."

Connor comes back into the studio. "Great news, guys. Despite that little mishap earlier, I got the perfect photos for the magazine."

My eyes light up as Connor shows us the pictures he took. They are beyond perfect. Even the pictures of Jett and me right before I ran into the bathroom.

"These photos are perfect, Connor," I gush.

"Thank you for letting me work with this beautiful woman," Jett says to Connor before smiling at me. Connor then smiles at me.

"I won't be surprised if this issue sells like hotcakes," Connor says. "You two are magic together."

"Thank you," I say to Connor. "And thank you, Jett, for making me feel at ease even if I didn't realize at first that's what you were trying to do."

We all hang around and chat together a little more before I say I have to leave, thanking them for the opportunity.

"Take care of yourself," Jett says as I'm heading out the door

I stop and wave to both of them. "I will."

ILLICIT DOSE OF SCARS

NINE

Journee

My dad said he'll be here around noon, and I'm so thankful I got everything out of the way. I finished all my shopping, stocking up on the essentials. I also cleaned the mess out of our apartment, so there really is nothing left for me to do but wait for him to arrive. I already did my daily search for modeling gigs earlier this morning, and I found a few that I booked for next week. I'm building my portfolio one gig at a time, so grateful to the photographers who keep my name on their lists. A few of them have called me back for other photoshoots.

I get dressed around ten and do a last-minute survey of the apartment before I decide to text Knox to see what he's doing. I miss him and can't wait until he gets home. I'm going to jump his bones as soon as he walks through our door.

Hey, babe. I miss you. How's it going? How have the concerts been? The crowds? I'm so proud of you and the band. You've come a long way. I can't wait to see you.

I go into the living room to watch some TV. I figure that will entertain me while I wait for my dad to come. I flip through the channels, but see nothing that sparks my interest, so I just turn to the music channel. I get a couple of texts from Knox a few minutes later.

Knox: *Hey, beautiful! The concerts are going well. The crowds have been huge and very welcoming.*

Knox: *Is your father there yet? Tell him I said hi. I'm counting down the days until I'm in your arms again. I fucking miss your body on mine. I love you.*

I quickly respond back, and as soon as I'm about to close out the text app, one from my dad pops up. He's stuck in traffic, but only about twenty minutes away. Lunch-time traffic is the worst. At least he's not too far away. I hope my dad sees the effort Knox and I put into decorating the apartment.

The doorbell rings after a while, sooner than I thought it would. The traffic must have eased up a lot. I make my way to the door and take a deep breath before opening it. There stands my dad, all six feet of him. He's dressed in sweats and sneakers, his short beard tapered and shaped up. He looks good. I guess he really needed the move. At one point I regretted not going with him, apprehensive about living on my own, but I'm glad I stayed.

"Hey, Dad. Looking good," I say, reaching for him to give him a hug.

"You're not looking too bad yourself," he says,

embracing me. "I missed you."

"Is your suitcase still in the car?"

"Yes. I'll get it later. I want to see this apartment of yours."

"Okay. Well, come on in," I say, leading the way into the apartment.

My dad wipes his feet on our welcome mat before stepping inside. "Nice apartment," he says, looking around. "You and Knox decorated it together, right?"

"Yes. We did," I say as I show him wall paintings Knox and I picked out. "Are you thirsty? I just went shopping for food. I wanted to make sure we had enough food in the apartment so we don't have to eat out."

"Water is fine," he says, taking a seat on our couch.

I grab two bottles of water from the kitchen, and I'm surprisingly nervous. My hands are sweaty, so much so I almost drop one of the bottles on the way back into the living room. I hand one to my dad and sit down next to him.

"So what's up? How have you been?" I ask as I unscrew the cap of my bottle and take a swig.

"Good. I've been good. Working a lot. How have you been?"

"I've been good. Also working a lot. I actually booked a few gigs for next week," I say proudly. I don't want him worrying about me. I'm old enough to take care of myself, and Knox has been nothing but supportive of me. I don't want my dad to have any reason to think I can't fend for myself.

"That's great, Journee," he says, smiling. "How's

everything going with you and Knox?"

"It's going great," I answer, hoping he doesn't ask any more questions about Knox.

"I'm glad to hear that. He made a good first impression on me when you invited him over for dinner that one time."

I don't respond. I just smile back, knowing if I told him about the "incident," he'd be more than pissed at Knox. He'd probably kill him. Maybe I'm making light of what happened, but Knox was high *and* drunk. And he did give me time to trust him again, which is why I decided to give him another chance. But no need to tell my dad about that. Knox and I worked it out privately.

My dad shifts back and forth on the couch, like he's contemplating whether to mention something on his mind. He takes a swig of his water before just staring down at the bottle, playing with the cap.

"Dad," I say, breaking the awkward silence. "Are you okay? You seem nervous." "I'm fine. I just wanted to tell you that I met someone," he says, still fidgeting with the bottle cap.

"Oh . . ."

He looks up at me in anticipation. "And you're okay with this?"

I decide to be honest. "Well . . . that was fast. Mom passed away a few months ago. But I understand you wanting to move on and find love again."

"Thank you for understanding. We met at work, and she's really a sweet woman. Her name is Pearl, and she's a widow herself. Her husband died in a car accident about two years ago. She has one son, who's twenty-three. His name is Sawyer."

"I'm happy you found someone. Really. It seems like you two have some things in common, which is good."

"Yes, we do. One day, you'll have to meet. Maybe you and her son could become friends . . . maybe even more than friends?" he suggested

"Dad, you know I'm dating Knox and we live together, right?" I say, reminding him. "I know, I know. I'm just saying if you two don't work out for whatever reason . . ." He chuckles lightly.

I knew deep down he despised Knox for taking me away from him. My dad blamed Knox, seeing my decision to stay here as me choosing my boyfriend over him. But what the hell? It's a little late to feel salty about it. Now I'm under the impression the only reason he came to visit is to get me to go back with him—and date a guy who could potentially be my step-brother if you marries this woman. Fuck no.

"Knox and I are okay, truthfully. I don't plan on leaving him. So you can get whatever plot you are trying to devise out of your mind," I say, kind of annoyed with him.

"I'm sorry. I know I overstepped my boundaries with that one, but I was just—" He cuts himself off when I flash my eyes at him. "Okay, okay. I get it."

"Thank you. Now, are you hungry?" I ask, changing the subject. "I can make hamburgers and fries if you like."

"Getting all domesticated, I see." he says jokingly. "That sounds good."

Who is this guy, and what has he done with my father? He sure has changed since he left. I don't know if I like this version of him. He certainly wasn't like this when my mom was still around. He was more reserved and modest in speech. It's like whoever this woman my dad is dating is influencing him to be more bold and unfiltered. I don't know what to make of it. But these sly remarks, especially trying to play matchmaker, is a definite no.

I quickly whip up two hamburgers and put some fries in the air fryer. After the food's done, I call my dad into the kitchen. We sit at the table and eat in silence. I think my dad is now realizing how dumb he sounded when he suggested I become "friends" with his girlfriend's son.

"I'm sorry," he says, breaking the silence between us.

I swallow the fry I'm chewing on. "It's okay."

"No. It's not. I shouldn't have suggested what I did, knowing full well you have Knox," he continues.

"Yeah. You shouldn't have, but I forgive you."

The week flew by, uneventful. My dad and I spent it mostly catching up. I was grateful that he came to visit for company since Knox was away, but this visit was sort of strange. He basically has a new life where he's living. It's like I don't matter to him as much anymore.

Maybe I'm jumping to conclusions, but it seems like his new girlfriend and her son have taken top priority.

They were the topic of conversation the whole week, even when I tried updating him on my life.

I'm pulled back to the present when Knox texts me, saying he will be walking through the door any minute now. It's been three weeks since I had sex. I am horny as fuck, so he's going to get what's coming to him once he enters our apartment. I'm purposely wearing my lacy boy shorts and polka dot top for the simple fact of wanting to turn him on.

After a few minutes, I hear the door unlock. Knox steps into our apartment, looking like a snack ready to be devoured, and I come out to greet him.

"Damn, girl. Someone's ready to play!" he teases, looking me up and down.

I coax him letting go of his suitcase and leaving it on the ground. Then I pull him toward me and crash into his mouth. Knox kisses me back, trailing his hands along my body. He picks me up and carries me to our bedroom before laying me on our bed.

"It's been three whole damn weeks. I'm going to fuck you into oblivion," he whispers to me while he strips. He purposely takes his time undressing me. I stare at his dick, hungrily wanting him to do what he promised. But as soon as I'm stark naked, I sit up.

Knox gives me a puzzled look. "What the hell?"

"Can I taste you first?" I ask coyly.

He has no objections, standing up for me. I kneel in front of him and begin sucking on his rock-hard shaft. I start off slowly to easy him into my rhythm, but I speed up after a while.

"Shit," Knox moans, playing with my curls.

When he finally comes into my mouth, I swallow all the ooey goodness that is him.

He smirks down at me. "Okay. My turn."

I lie down, Knox climbing on top of me. He kisses me wildly, and I kiss him back with that same passion. He finally slides into me, and it's like all my pent-up frustration from the last three weeks disappears.

After several hours of making up for lost time, we both collapse on the bed next to each other. Rapidly breathing, we stare at the ceiling, then look at each other and laugh.

"What the hell was that, Journee? That was fucking amazing!" Knox says, trying to catch his breath.

"Blame it on me being extra horny from the lack of sex these past three weeks," I say, laughing.

Knox shakes his head in disbelief. "Maybe I should deprive your ass even when I'm not away so you can be like this more often."

I give him a stern look. "You wouldn't!"

"Try me."

"Fuck you."

He laughs. "I'm only joking, Journee. Chill."

I quickly sit up, hyperventilating. For a brief moment, the "incident" flashes before my eyes . . . I have to calm down.

"Are you okay? Babe?" He's staring at me now.

"I'm fine," I lie.

Even though I forgave him, Knox never really acknowledged what he did to me. Yes, he said he didn't remember what happened, but he had to remember *something*. He couldn't have been so fucked up that he couldn't remember anything, right?

"So my dad came to visit while you were away," I tell him, diverting the conversation.

"Oh? How did that go?" he asks.

"It went okay. He met someone, and that was most of the conversation while he was here," I say somberly.

"I'm guessing you're not happy about that."

"I thought I could accept it, but he totally wasn't listening to me when I wanted to discuss what was going on in my life. It was like my life didn't matter to him anymore."

"Journee, I hate to say it, but you weren't actually happy that your dad moved. He just wanted to share his happiness with you so you would know he didn't move out of spite. Just like you're happy here, he's happy with his new life."

"I guess. I'm just a little disappointed that his new girlfriend and her son are taking priority over me, his daughter," I explain.

My dad's new life is bothering me. I thought I would be fine with it, but this is all happening too fast. My mom just passed away. Doesn't her memory mean anything to him? Maybe his girlfriend reminds him of Mom and he reminds this lady of her husband. It's going to take some getting used to, but I have no choice. Lost in my own thoughts, I decide to take a shower. After getting dressed I head into the kitchen to make breakfast, noticing Knox on the phone as I leave the bedroom.

"Journee," Knox calls out, probably wondering where I ran off to.

"I'm making breakfast for us," I yell back.

Knox enters the kitchen and grabs me by my waist. He starts kissing my neck. "Thanks, babe."

"Who was that you were talking to?" I ask curiously.

"You remember Seth, our band manager? He wants us to shoot a music video. He thinks that will build up more hype for the band."

"That's so awesome. It would definitely get the fans going. Visuals are everything."

"Seth wants to meet with us in an hour to go over the concept," Knox explains.

"Oh, all right. I'm almost finished with breakfast."

I'm just finishing up making the pancakes. Although I don't cook every day, ever since I started learning how to cook, I've been making full legit meals for Knox.

"It's no rush, babe. I can be a little late." He smiles and kisses my forehead before we sit down to eat. "Thanks again. I really appreciate you."

"You're welcome. I figured you must be famished after that good fuck I gave you," I smirked.

"Damn right, I am!" Knox exclaims.

We continue talking about what Seth has in mind for the music video concept—I'm so proud of Knox and his band—until he has to leave. He kisses me lightly on the lips before he heads out the door, while I pout.

TEN

Knox

The meeting with Seth lasted longer than we had all expected. Journee already texted me, asking where I was. There was so much to go over as far as logistics went. Dorian and Phoenix, the director and photographer, were also there. They, along with Seth, wanted to make sure everything was in place for the shoot.

I walk into the apartment to find the TV on some random reality show and Journee asleep on the couch. I decide to let her get her sleep while I make dinner. It's the least I can do after she made breakfast this morning. I go into the kitchen to see what we had that I could make for dinner. I want to make something simple and easy, nothing too complicated, but something we both are in the mood for. After rummaging through the cabinets, fridge, and freezer, I pull out some ground turkey, to make turkey meatloaf, and potatoes and broccoli for the sides.

I'm not as skilled in the kitchen as Journee despite living on my own for a few years now. But I recently decided it wouldn't be fair to Journee if I had her cook all the time. So I looked up a few recipes online and experimented with them. The first few times I cooked for Journee, it was touch and go for a minute. My ass had no clue what the hell I was doing, but I was grateful she wasn't too critical of my skills—or lack of. But I've gotten a lot better, to be honest. Now Journee can stomach what I make.

The smell of food drifts through the apartment, and I'm thankful it actually smells edible.

"What smells so good up in here?" Journee says, walking into the kitchen.

"I'm making turkey meatloaf, broccoli, and potatoes," I say proudly.

"Oh, shit. My man's cooking," she smirks. "You must want some extra bedroom brownie points."

"I'll take anything I can get."

"Seriously. Thanks, babe." Journee hugs me from behind.

"Our meeting went well, by the way."

"That's wonderful."

"Would you like to be in our music video?" I ask. "I would love you to. I don't want any random girl to be hugging up on me."

"I wouldn't feel too comfortable with you cozying up to some random chick either. Of course I'll be in your music video. When are you guys aiming to shoot the video?"

"In two weeks. Seth has to talk with the director to finalize the date and time of the shoot," I explain.

"Sounds fun."

"The concept is so cool. We FaceTimed with Dorian at the meeting, and he had this dopeass idea. He wants to combine our vintage concert footage with our recent shows. The parts that we would actually be filming for the shoot would be like a sneak peak of us practicing or getting ready for a gig. Remember Willow and Sarai? You guys'll be in the video to support us," I explain.

Journee and I settle down to eat, though I secretly want her to be serious about those bedroom brownie points. I'm a guy. I can't help if I need Journee like she's the only girl I have left to fuck in the entire world. I'm consumed by her presence, and being inside her wards off every depressive and anxious thought drugs alone can't fix.

We're shooting the music video shoot at the Pavilion. Not only does the Pavilion have studio rooms, it also has a few open large rooms specifically for music videos. Seth reserved the space for two days. Journee and I arrive at the Pavilion around nine in the morning. Dorian, the director, and Seth are talking with Phoenix, who's acting as our behind-the-scenes photographer. They're probably going over the schedule and everything. Ezra, Willow, Reid, and Sarai are sitting down, eating the breakfast Dorian provided. Journee and I grab what we want before joining them.

"You guys ready?" Dorian says after we're basically done eating.

"Let's rock and roll," Ezra says excitedly.

Reid and I both go to our instruments, while Ezra stands in front of his microphone. We're doing the "live performance" portion of the video. We perform a new song we're working on. Journee, Willow, and Sarai stand to the side, cheering us on like the supportive girlfriends they are. Me, I'm playing for Journee and only Journee, and she knows it. She gives me purpose, puts meaning behind everything I do in the band. It's not just about making it as a band or becoming famous. It's now for her. I do this for her.

Phoenix is moving around, taking photos as we jam out. He apparently took pictures of us while we were eating earlier too. Then again, he's here to get all the action behind the scenes. After taking a few shots of us, he points his camera toward Journee, Willow, and Sarai. I can't help but be a tad bit jealous of him as he's snaps pictures of Journee.

I can't help but imagine them as a couple. I mean, he's a photographer, and she's a model.

It would be like a match made in heaven. Wait. The hell? No, it wouldn't. What the fuck am I on right now? If I ever lost Journee, I'd go batshit crazy. Especially to him . . . Oh, hell no. Calm down. I gotta calm down. I can feel anger sweeping over me. It's hot all of a sudden, and I'm starting to sweat. Reid and Ezra glance my way.

"Are you okay?" Reid mouths, still drumming.

"I need a break," I mouth back.

"Dorian, can we take ten?" Ezra yells.

Dorian calls for a break. I gently place my guitar on its stand. I rush to Journee, take her by the hand, and lead her into a side room. I can feel everyone's eyes on us, so I shut the door and lock it behind us.

"Do you love me?" I ask Journee frantically.

Her eyes widen. "Why are you asking me this? Are you okay?"

"I need to know you love me and will never leave me."

"I won't. You know that."

"Prove it," I demand. "We have ten minutes."

"How?"

"Fuck me."

"What? Here? Now? You *do* realize there are people outside this door, and we are at your music video shoot, for God's sakes," she tries to reason.

"I don't give a shit. You will do as I say."

I push her against the wall and unbutton her jeans. I pull them down along with her panties, down to her feet. My jeans and boxers go next. Then I fuck her against the wall.

There's a knock on the door after a while, and I can hear Seth talking. "Knox, we have to finish up the shoot."

"Okay, yeah. Give us a couple more minutes," I yell back at him.

I casually get dressed like I didn't just force myself on my girlfriend. Damn. I fucked up again, and this time, I wasn't high *or* drunk. Journee looks at me with utter despair.

"I just needed to know you loved me," I whisper to her.

Journee casts her eyes to the floor, a single tear

rolling down her cheek. "I love you," she says, but I know it's out of desperation.

Journee

I leave the room, feeling like shit. But what the fuck was I supposed to do? This is the band's music video shoot. I wasn't going to make a scene, and I certainly don't want to embarrass Knox in front of everyone. So I'm going to bite my tongue and remain resolute, unwavering.

When Knox and I reappear, Seth asks, "Are you guys okay?"

"Yeah. Cool. Everything's cool," Knox says as he watches me sit with Willow and Sarai.

Willow turns to me when I plop down next to her. "Hey, girl is everything okay?"

"Yes. It's fine." I stare at Knox, who's chatting it up with his bandmates.

"You guys were in there for a bit," Sarai says, concerned

"We were just . . . talking."

Willow raises her eyebrow. "Talking?? Hmm . . . if you say so."

I shoot her a look and grit my teeth. "That's what we were doing."

"Okay, okay. Sorry I even asked."

We watch the boys finish the video shoot without

calling us over to make cameos. But I don't mind. I don't feel up to being in the video anyway, not after what just took place. While we sit, waiting for them to wrap it up, I look around the Pavilion, wondering what else the band's practices consisted of. They aren't shy about letting people know they smoke weed and drink alcohol during practices. But what other things go on during their rehearsals? Are the guys being faithful to us? Or are they fucking other girls behind our backs? I accidentally lock eyes with the photographer. He looks back at me with such intent, like he isn't looking at me, but into my battered soul. I quickly look away. What the hell? Do I wear my pain? Can people tell?

"Let's go to Drinks On Me," Dorian suggests. The boys quickly agree.

"Are you girls up for going?" Knox asks us.

Willow and Sarai answer enthusiastically. I don't say anything at first, so everyone's staring at me, awaiting my answer like it really matters in the whole scheme of things. They would have went with or without me. I'm not even drinking age. What fun would I have, watching them all get wasted? But I don't want to be the party pooper.

"Yeah. Let's go," I finally answer.

"Great. Let's finish up here. Then we'll head over," Dorian states.

Everyone heads to their respective cars after cleanup. Inside Knox's car, I put my seatbelt on and sit in silence, staring out the window. I don't have anything to say to Knox, and I have to refrain from letting my tears drop. He knows what to do to break me every fucking time. And every time, like an idiot, I forgive him. Maybe I secretly like being tortured by him. Maybe he really does own me and can do whatever the fuck he wants.

"Journee, I'm sorry," Knox says finally, breaking the silent tension between us.

"Fuck you," I say angrily.

"I deserved that."

"Why?"

"I don't know why."

"You don't know why you always force me . . ." My words falter as I choke up.

Knox doesn't respond. He just keeps his eyes on the road. I don't get him sometimes. I know he loves me, and I just want to understand. It's not like we don't have sex almost on a regular basis. We do. So I don't know what his problem is.

Once we arrive at Drinks On Me Restaurant & Bar, I get out of the car and start walking to the entrance, but Knox grabs my arm and pulls me in for an embrace.

"Babe, please. I fucked up. I'm an asshole. I'm begging you. Please forgive me."

"I . . . I . . ." I start to say, but my words don't come out.

"Shh," Knox whispers before kissing my forehead.

Fucking A. There's that hold Knox has on me. Maybe if I knew more people… But really, who am I kidding? I always end up convincing myself he's not *that* bad.

We enter the restaurant hand in hand. Knox grabs a table for us, and I immediately start looking though the menu. I'm starving. Buffalo chicken wings with ranch and a Shirley Temple sound real good, but I don't want to order before everyone else gets here. Knox leaves, and comes back with the others a few minutes later.

"I'm so hungry," Willow tells Ezra.

"I'll ask for more menus," Ezra replies.

"Are you sure you're okay?" Willow whispers to me.

"Yeah, I'm fine." I'm really not fine. I need an escape, a way to leave before Willow starts asking me more questions. The bathroom. I can hide away there for a few minutes to collect my thoughts.

"I'm going to use the restroom," I abruptly say to Willow.

"Do you want me to come with you?"

"No."

I enter the restroom, lock myself in one of the stalls, and start to cry. How stupid am I? Knox is using me for his own pleasure, and he feels no remorse about it. This is the second time he's done this to me. When is enough enough? I wipe my eyes with the toilet tissue and wash my hands. Sarai is at the sink and notices me next to her.

"Journee, what's wrong? Why are your eyes so puffy?" she asks curiously. "Were you crying?"

I stutter an incoherent response.

"Did something happen today?" she continues. "After you came out of that room, you weren't the same." My tears spill over and flow down my face like a river escaping a dam.

Sarai hugs me and whispers in my ear. "I'm here

for you if you want to talk about it."

I slowly pull away from her. Does she know? But Sarai just lets go of me and says nothing else as she finishes washing her hands.

She leaves the bathroom before me. I decide to linger back a little. As soon as I felt I could leave the bathroom, I return to the group and sit next to Knox. Reid hands Sarai a menu, which she thumbs through. Knox puts his hand on my thigh and rubs it. My body tenses, and I look around to see if anyone notices. Sarai glances up from her menu and gives me a reassuring look. I give her a half-smile in return.

"We were just discussing the timeline for when the video will be ready to upload to the band's YouTube channel," Dorian says.

"When will that be?" Knox says, curious.

"It should be good to go in two weeks, ready to upload in about a month," Seth answers.

"Oh, that's not too long."

"No, it's not, and I should have the behind-the-scenes photos ready in about that time as well," Phoenix adds. "I'll give the photos to Seth to put on the website to coincide with the release of the music video."

"That's perfect," Ezra says, excited. "That'll definitely create some buzz for the music video."

"Let's toast." Dorian raises his beer glass. Everyone else follows suit. "To millions of YouTube views and the band's success!"

"Here, here." Seth clanks his glass against Dorian's.

The rest of us toast and take a drink at the same

time. I'm so proud of Knox and his band. I may not have been there since the beginning, but just seeing them grow their fanbase . . . and now a music video? Such a great accomplishment!

Our food arrives after a while. As I'm eating, I feel someone's eyes on me. I glance up to find the photographer staring straight at me. It's a little creepy. This is the second time today I've caught him staring. What's his problem? I don't want to be rude, since he's the band's photographer, but what the fuck? Knox is eating when he gets wind of Phoenix staring at me.

That's when Phoenix looks away.

ILLICIT DOSE OF SCARS

ELEVEN

Knox

As soon as Journee and I reach the apartment, I go straight to the living room to turn the TV on. Journee decides to take a shower and get more comfortable before we watch a movie. Flipping through the channels, I try to find something decent to watch. Journee isn't picky; she's pretty much down to watch anything. I settled on *The Avengers*. It's set to start in ten minutes, so I head into the bedroom to change into something more comfortable myself.

Journee is already out of the shower by the time I enter. She's putting on what she typically likes to lounge around in. This usually consists of one of my oversized hoodies, and yoga pants. Journee puts her hair up in a high, messy bun. She turns around from the mirror when she sees my reflection.

"You look sexy as hell," I compliment her.

She blushes and continue fixing her hair in the mirror. I go through the closet and change into sweats and a T-shirt, Journee slyly watching.

"Like what you see?" I tease her.

"Oh, yeah," she teases back.

We head back into the living room. Journee sits on the couch, and I tell her that she can start the movie as I head to the kitchen.

"Do you want any popcorn?"

"That's fine," she replies. "Did you have fun at our music video shoot?" I ask her when I come back with the popcorn.

"Yeah. It was nice to experience what goes on behind the scenes. It was also awesome to catch up with Willow and Sarai."

"I'm sorry that you girls weren't in the video itself, like we planned. It was a last-minute change."

"It was no problem. Just being there to witness the shoot was fine by me."

I'm taken aback by her nonchalant answer. I love having Journee there by my side, but I didn't expect jealousy would fuel my rage, causing me to hurt her yet again. I know there's no need to be jealous of Phoenix, but I can't help it. The way he's looked at her a few times in the past, it made my blood boil. It was a matter of time before it came to a head. The first time I snapped, I was high and intoxicated. It was partly Journee's fault for not being there, and partly Laney's fault for seducing me. But it was also the demons of my past haunting me.

The movie starts, and I pull Journee close to me. She lays her head on my shoulder and closes her eyes. I start playing with her hair. She's so naive and innocent, always putting up with my constant bullshit. It's really not fair to her. But as sick and twisted as it sounds, I don't want her with anyone else. So if I have to keep her broken enough to stay with me, I will. Because as soon as she realizes she's better off without me, I'm screwed. She can't escape. I won't let her.

Seeing her broken hurts the shit out of me, but it's the only way she won't run.

ACKNOWLEDGEMENTS

Kimberly See
Your comments and suggestions during the editing process of "Illicit Dose Of Scars," helped a great deal to make my book better than it originally was. So thank you.

Diana TC
Thank you so much for making me another EPIC cover design for "Illicit Dose Of Scars."

Samantha La Mar (TalkNerdy2Me)
Thank you so much for the amazing chapter designs that you did for "Illicit Dose Of Scars."

Mackenzie (NiceGirlNaughtyEdits)
Thank you so much for making the teasers for "Illicit Dose Of Scars." I loved them so much!

Family and Friends
Thank you so much for the continued support of me and my books. I love you all.

Regina Ann Faith *is a Lyricist, Poet, Writer, Composer and Author. She graduated with a B.A in Communications/Film. This is her first dark romance series titled The Love Sick Series. The first book in this series titled Illicit Dose Of Scars follows the toxic relationship between Journee, an aspiring model and Knox, a guitarist who is abusive and controlling. She also has another two book series titled "The Artistic Series."*

She can be found on her social media pages at:

www.facebook.com/AuthorReginaAnnFaith
www.twitter.com/ReginaAnnFaith
www.instagram.com/ReginaAnnFaith
www.soundcloud.com/ReginaAnnFaith
www.youtube.com/ReginaAnnFaithMusic